Changing
Faces

TAKE ONE

Changing Faces

WENDY LAWTON

MOODY PUBLISHERS
CHICAGO

All Scripture quotations are taken from the *Holy Bible, New International
Version*®. NIV®. Copyright © 1973, 1978, 1984 by International Bible
Society. Used by permission of Zondervan Publishing House. All rights
reserved.

Library of Congress Cataloging-in-Publication Data

Lawton, Wendy.
    Changing faces / by Wendy Lawton.
        p. cm. — (Real TV—real transformations series ; Take 1)
    Summary: Seventeen-year-old Olivia, an "overscheduled" honor
student who is trying to find time for friends, family, God, homework,
and volunteering at a homeless shelter, receives the startling news that
she has been chosen to receive a beauty makeover on the reality
television show, "Changing Faces."
    ISBN 0-8024-5413-5
    [1. Interpersonal relations—Fiction. 2. Shelters for the homeless—
Fiction. 3. Conduct of life—Fiction. 4. Christian life—Fiction.] I. Title.

PZ7.L4425Ch 2004
[Fic]—dc22

                                                               2004002826

                            1 3 5 7 9 10 8 6 4 2

                    Printed in the United States of America

For Diane

So many milestones on your journey inspired me—
from valedictorian to cancer survivor and beyond.

Contents

Acknowledgments

Special thanks to my seventeen-year-old daughter, Rae Lynn, who is living her frenetic senior year while I write this book. Over many a mocha frappuccino at our bookstore, she helped me develop the book, name the characters, and play with scenes. She willingly sat with me through hours of makeover television programs and, without a word of protest, helped me do research at Sephora. What a trouper!

And a tip of the hat to The Learning Channel, Style Network, and BBC television programs that spawned the concept for the Real TV series. For *Changing Faces*, I spent serious couch time watching *Fashion Emergency!*, *Date Patrol*, *What Not to Wear*, and my all-time favorite, *A Second Look*. The creators of these programs—despite the fun and fluff—actually take the concept of makeover much deeper.

And, as always, big thanks to the incomparable editorial and design team at Moody Publishing; to my agent, Janet Grant; and to Crystal Miller, who read the manuscript in advance.

Real TV

It Only

1

It's time for *Changing Faces,* Olivia. Turn on the TV; I'm on my way." *Click.*

Olivia O'Donnell didn't even have time to answer before Jane hung up. She knew that her best friend was probably already backing her Jetta down her driveway. Olivia looked at her watch—four minutes flat, she guessed. Jane lived about a half mile away. *OK, I have just enough time to rout Sherman out of the family room.*

"Tank," she yelled, pulling off one earpiece of his headphones, "I'm on Dad's TV chart for this hour—*Changing Faces.*"

"I'm almost to the next level, Olivia."

Though only twelve, her brother Sherman managed to take up the whole couch when he spread out. At five feet ten and nearing 150 pounds, he was hard to ignore. Dad joked that they named him after Mom's side of the family—the Shermans—not after the famous tank.

"Please. Just a few more minutes?"

"Good try, Tank, but you know how Mom is." She adopted her best mom look, placing her hands on her hips and using that slow exasperated voice Mom always used when dealing with disagreements. "We negotiated this schedule, and we all agreed to stick to it."

"Rats. Why can't we be like other families? All my friends have their own TVs and get to keep their gaming stuff in their bedroom." He picked up his deck and the equipment spread out over the coffee table, stuffing it into the basket in the entertainment center. Every bit of his twelve-year-old angst showed in his parting comment, "It would be *so* nice to live in a normal family."

Olivia ignored him as he trudged upstairs. Neither one of them liked the media restrictions. It took all the spontaneity out of television and video. And Tank never even attempted to compete with his friends on Internet games. He'd barely get a team put together and he'd have to log off. Of course, as much as it irritated her, Olivia understood the reason why her parents were so tight about TV, gaming, movies, and the like. Some of her friends watched two or three hours of television a day—even more in the summer. As Mom said, it could eat up hours. Olivia knew that part of the reason she was almost certain to be named valedictorian was because, much of the time, homework was the most exciting thing to do in her house.

". . . And he swerved and I just missed him, but I'm here." Jane opened the door midsentence. "I cannot believe I'm late. Turn on the TV, for goodness' sake." Jane never stopped talking. She bubbled with enthusiasm, and it just sort of spilled out of her mouth. Today her blonde hair was scrunched into a clip. Olivia loved the way Jane had natural highlights. Most girls had to resort to peroxide to get what Jane had naturally. When they first met, Jane barely had a freckleless spot on her face, but now she had only a sprinkle of light freckles across her nose—just enough to make her look outdoorsy. She could cover them completely if she wanted, with a light dusting of powder.

"I had to kick Tank off the tube first. Here." The television clicked on with a whirring sound. Olivia already had her channel programmed into the favorites. *Click.*

". . . another exciting episode of *Changing Faces.*" The theme music faded as the announcer's intro ended.

"Yikes! I can't believe what Kinni is wearing today. My mom would kill me. Besides, don't you think it makes her hips look wide?" Jane always commented throughout the entire show.

Good thing I'm a multitasker. Olivia looked at her friend as she talked. *I wonder if I like* Changing Faces *for itself or if it's the combination of* Changing Faces *and Jane Broga?*

"Those rhinestone flip-flops would sure get noticed here, wouldn't they?" Jane said. "I can just see them!" Jane giggled. They both grew up in Bay Vista, a suburb located to the east of San Francisco Bay. In the nineties, the famed Silicon Valley crept north to include their once-quiet community.

"I know. They'd get noticed here." Olivia muted the

commercial. "When online friends hear I live in California, they always picture Hollywood or Southern California—definitely the rhinestone flip-flop portion of the state." She laughed. "Bay Vista's more like the Birkenstock part of the state."

"Sad but true." Jane probably would have liked to try rhinestone flip-flops. It didn't take people long to find out that she was certainly no plain Jane.

Jane had talked her way into Olivia's life in kindergarten, and they'd been friends ever since. There was nothing like a friend who remembered watching you hanging on the chain-link fence, crying for your mommy. It sure kept one from reinventing oneself with any conviction.

Olivia wished she could be more spontaneous and as much fun as her friend, but she was the one always described as a good student. When she read the comments people wrote in last year's yearbook, she counted no less than twenty "nice" and "sweet" descriptions of her. *Boring.*

"Do you want something to drink?" Olivia jumped up to take advantage of the last minutes of the commercial break before the next segment of the show.

"Got any of those juice-y things your mom buys?"

"Sure." She unscrewed the lids in the kitchen and debated only a minute about whether to pour the drinks into glasses. Why dirty glasses when you could just as easily drink straight from the bottle?

". . . And they are making over a teacher? Eeeuuuwww. I can't believe school starts on Monday. I can guarantee none of our teachers will be sporting a makeover. Where did summer—"

"Here comes the part when they show the secret

14

camera footage." Olivia always cringed in sympathy for the embarrassed guest. The host, Kinni McKay, did a voice-over as the screen flashed with the before-shots of the guest. Luckily, *Changing Faces* was not like some of the reality TV shows that actually put a hidden camera on the trail of the person. *Changing Faces* used still photography collected secretly by the guest's friends—or rather, so-called friends.

"I'd love to be on the show." Jane took a long slurp of her drink. "But I'd die if you submitted ugly snapshots. I wonder if you could use semigood photos. . . ."

"The fun is contrasting the woof-woofness of the initial photos against the glam shots at the end." Olivia loved the idea of makeover—why was that? "Gross! Look at that orangey lipstick."

"She's actually not bad for a teacher," Jane said as the before-shots faded out. "They should have gotten Harvey." Jane shook her head and sighed. "Now that would be some makeover!"

"You're bad." Olivia enjoyed Jane's outrageous comments, knowing she never meant harm. "Ms. Harvey probably spends so much time on her lesson plans that she barely finds time to run a comb through her hair."

"And obviously no time to apply makeup."

"But, admit it," Olivia said, using her no-nonsense look that drove Jane mad. "You could sit through three solid hours of her class and never once look at your watch."

"OK, I'll admit it, but if you didn't get so caught up in her teaching, she'd be hard to look at day after day." Jane pointed to the screen. "Look at the outfit she's trying on. Can you imagine a teacher wearing a suede blazer with cool pants like that?"

"I wonder if she'll choose that one?"

The premise of the show was simple—Kinni McKay introduced the makeover subject by showing the before-photos submitted by friends. Then Kinni would show up at the guest's workplace and somehow surprise her with a huge check for clothing and tickets to Hollywood, inviting her to "change faces." Of course, the show involved more than a cosmetic makeover. Fashion, posture, hair, accessories—all came under scrutiny.

"Can you imagine? A shopping spree in L.A.?" Jane always talked through this part. Of course, she talked through all the parts. "I'd choose Rodeo Drive, at least for one tiny accessory, just to say I'd shopped there."

"Not me. I'd pick the secondhand shops on Melrose Avenue."

"Do you think they'd let you keep your vintage look? I'll bet they'd take your hair and razor-cut it in spiky sections. And the hair colorist would say, 'That brown is positively mousy.'"

"So now it comes out. You think my hair is mousy, don't you?" Olivia was teasing, although Jane often unwittingly let her feelings escape in the sheer mass of words.

"No." Jane stopped looking at the television. "No, I was just repeating what they would say. I like your mousy brown hair, girlfriend."

Olivia hit her with one of the floor pillows. "Spoken by a blonde! My hair happens to be a sophisticated ash brown. Very chic. Very understated."

"Look." Jane smiled her I-told-you-so smile as she watched the *Changing Faces* hairstylist hand the teacher over to the colorist.

"Can't you do something with this mousy brown

hair?" The stylist flipped a piece of the hair with apparent disdain.

"Ouch." Olivia laughed and hit Jane with another pillow. "That's too cruel."

"The hairstylist said it; I didn't."

Olivia's dog, Puggles, started barking. The noise saved Jane from getting bashed a third time with the pillow. Puggles was a cross between a pug and a beagle. When he wagged his tail, it wagged his whole body. With his big eyes, loose skin, and attitude, he melted hearts—but his voice—he had the bell-like voice of a beagle. Both girls ended up covering their ears.

"Puggles, chill."

When things finally settled back down, the two friends watched the rest of the hour-long show, interspersing each segment with their own running commentary. The best part of the show for Olivia was the part when they showed snippets of the guest's life. Seeing the teacher in her classroom and at home, Olivia could see that, although today's guest did benefit from a makeover, she needed no polishing in the classroom. This footage, scattered throughout the show, made the viewers connect with the guest much deeper than skin, nails, hair, and clothes.

In one of the *Changing Faces* fanzines, Olivia had read that they call this in-depth footage the B-roll.

Jane turned to Olivia as the credits rolled. "Brilliant! Lit-rally brilliant." Ever since Jane started watching the BBC reality TV shows, she'd adopted two Brit phrases— "brilliant"—always said with that upper crust hard *r* sound. Her other favorite was "fantastic," which sounded more like "fintastic."

Olivia laughed. Was anyone more fun than Jane Broga?

"No, I mean it. What a great makeover. She looked so different, and yet they didn't make her into a glamour queen. Seeing her in the classroom made the woman seem almost human. That's saying a lot for a teacher."

"You're awful, Jane! Is that any attitude to have? Especially on the last Tuesday before we start our senior year."

But Olivia agreed with Jane. The B-roll stuff made the show. *How sad is it that if I ever got a* Changing Faces *makeover, my B-roll footage would consist of watching me do homework, fighting with Tank, going to church, and doing the dinner dishes? Oh, yes, and slaving over my day planner to squeeze out just one more hour. Sheesh. What a life.*

Olivia shook her head. *Why am I scripting my B-roll? A guest on* Changing Faces—*how's that for an overactive imagination? If only . . .*

Moving the Goalposts

2

Did we ever luck out!" Jane leaned over and slapped a happy-face sticker on Olivia's notebook. "How long has it been since we sat together in homeroom?"

"What a cool way to end our school days," Olivia whispered back as the new teacher opened her laptop to take roll. "The very same way we began thirteen years ago."

"Yep, just like Aubrey still sits with all the guys." Jane nodded her head toward the back of the room and Olivia's lifelong nemesis.

"Some things never change." Aubrey's

cubby in kindergarten had sat between Olivia's and Jane's. Even then, Aubrey's pale blonde hair and blue eyes seemed to make her a boy magnet. By second grade, she'd learned to effectively bat those eyelashes and wind a meandering finger through those curls. And it only got worse as she got older. The curls gave way to long straight razor-trimmed hair, and the blonde went even paler in streaks over dark blonde.

Strangely enough, with Aubrey there always somehow seemed to be a competition thing with Olivia. Whenever Olivia ventured into her line of vision, Aubrey would crank up the charm, and the guys around her didn't stand a chance. It frustrated Olivia. *I'm not even into dating, let alone trophy dating.* She'd decided during the summer that this year she would not play the Aubrey competition game. *Why do I always let her set me off, anyway?*

"Olivia O'Donnell?" The teacher looked up to find her.

"Here." Olivia smiled.

Aubrey leaned over to one of her admirers and spoke in a loud stage whisper, "Notice Olivia's initials —O. O. That's what everyone says when they see her coming. Uh-oh." Aubrey wiggled her fingers and smirked at Olivia.

Olivia rolled her eyes. *That's the best she can do?*

"Aubrey, right?" The teacher glanced down at her laptop. "Aubrey Ainsley, I'd appreciate it if you didn't speak out in class." She took her glasses off and focused on Aubrey. "I was speaking to Olivia. Your interruption constitutes what I consider rude behavior." She put her glasses back on and flipped over a couple of pages in the handout on her desk. "Turn to page three of your handout titled 'Class Guidelines.' It addresses your infraction."

Aubrey made a face. Josh Higbee, obviously smitten by Aubrey, snickered. Anything Aubrey said or did seemed to charm Josh, no matter how lame.

It starts all over again. What makes me the perfect foil for Aubrey? Why did she choose me? Olivia pulled herself up in her seat. *Stop. Ignore her. You know she craves attention. Don't fall into that trap.*

Olivia opened her day planner to the section marked "Goals" as the teacher finished the lengthy first-day roll call.

Her list was fresh. She'd worked hard on her goals this summer. Staying focused—that was her mission. She already excelled at it, but this was her last year before college. More than ever, she needed to stay on task. She knew that a million distractions could crop up in the senior year. She wanted to finish well. *No, that's not true. I want to finish first.*

She read her list:

1. Daily Quiet Time. *Oops. Missed that this morning because of first-day craziness. Gotta get better.*
2. Clinch Valedictorian Standing. *Should be a piece of cake. Those two AP classes surely did the trick.*
3. Do Not Overschedule. *Well, so far, so good.* She had school, church, youth group, music lessons, tennis team, choir, study group for the final SATs, and . . .

"Don't forget to pencil me in." Jane leaned over and whispered with that evil grin of hers.

Olivia whacked her with a pencil. Jane always tortured Olivia about her day planner. Jane was a seat-of-the-pants-type girl. Olivia lived by systems. She could never accomplish half of what she accomplished if it weren't for her organizational skills.

As the teacher worked her way from *R* to *S*, Olivia took out her pencil and wrote: "4. Completely ignore Aubrey." *Hmmmm. That would be some accomplishment after thirteen years.* Olivia looked over at Aubrey. As usual, she had managed to seat herself in the middle of an adoring throng of guys. One, however, did not seem overly enthralled. In fact, he sat with his elbow on the desk and his head propped on his hand looking straight at Olivia.

Who is he? He must be new.

As if on cue, the teacher called, "Carter Wylie?"

He turned his attention away from Olivia and raised his hand.

"You transferred from . . ."

"Palo Alto."

Olivia could see Aubrey perk up. A new guy in town presented exactly the kind of challenge she loved. *Oops. There I go again. I need to stop reacting to her nonverbal bait. He's all yours, Aubrey. I've got too much in my day planner already.* She closed her planner as the teacher closed her laptop.

"I'm also new. My name is Mrs. Brenner. Thanks for your patience as I tried to connect faces with names." She looked around the room again as if mentally going over each student's name. "One last piece of business— I need to read the bulletin each Monday morning so we're all on the same page. Bear with me."

As she began to read some of the highlights, Olivia opened her day planner again to write down specific dates and events.

"Three-Way Tie for Valedictorian," Mrs. Brenner read.

Olivia's mouth went dry. What did it mean, "tie"? What about the AP classes?

"Despite the launch of AP classes last year, Bay Vista High still has three students vying for top spot." Mrs. Brenner looked around the room and connected with Olivia. "Congratulations, Olivia. I see you are one of the top three students."

Olivia tried to smile, but her mouth was so dry her lip caught on her teeth. It probably looked like a grimace. How could she have worked so hard and earned close to perfect grades and still be one of a pack of three?

"The announcement goes on to say that the panel may have to look to volunteer hours to break the tie." Mrs. Brenner put the bulletin down and picked up her class notes.

Just like that? Volunteerism? Olivia had spent the last three years slaving over her academics. Nobody had said a word about volunteer efforts. She looked down at her day planner. Where in the world was she supposed to fit in volunteer hours? There was nothing she hated more than someone changing the rules three-quarters into the game—it was like moving the goalposts.

"You OK?" Jane mouthed the words.

Olivia could only shake her head in exasperation as she drew a line through the center of goal number three: Do not overschedule. *So much for good intentions.* She was going to have to get herself a serious volunteer position to make up for three years of straight academics.

She struggled with focus the rest of the day—how could she work it all in and still have any kind of life?

✿   ✿   ✿

"Mom?" Olivia walked into the house just in time to set the table for dinner. After school she'd gone with Jane to get her school supplies. "Sorry I'm late. The lines at Staples went on forever. There must have been a hundred elementary school kids needing help."

"No problem. I just got home as well."

Her mom could pull together almost any dinner in thirty minutes or less. Good thing. Patty O'Donnell had a schedule that made Olivia's look tame. Her mom had logged over ten thousand miles with Meals on Wheels; she'd earned her one-gallon blood donor T-shirt twice; she worked at the reception desk of the hospital every Tuesday and Thursday; and she chaired the hospital auxiliary Christmas gala each year. And that didn't count her years as a Sunday school teacher.

"Will you throw together a quick Caesar salad, Olivia? There's a bag of prewashed romaine in the crisper, a jar of dressing in the fridge, garlic croutons in the bread drawer, and shaved parmesan in a bag in the deli drawer."

"Hmmmm. What's that saying? The apple doesn't fall far from the tree?" Olivia opened the lettuce into the bowl and put four salad plates in the freezer to chill.

"What are you talking about?"

"Jane and my other friends kid me about my day planner and my organization systems." Olivia poured dressing over the romaine and began tossing the leaves. "I can see where I get it from."

Mom laughed. "You were born organized. While other toddlers threw their blocks around the room, you were sorting them by color and size." She slipped

24

the split loaves of garlic bread under the broiler and drained the pasta into a colander in the sink.

"I may be organized, but this year is going to test me to the max. You know what I've wanted more than anything, right?"

"As if anyone could not know, Ms. Valedictorian."

"I know, I've probably put too much emphasis on it, but I'm all about excellence—it's not a competition thing, you know." Olivia wondered why she always felt defensive as she put words to her dream.

"Dad and I are proud of you. We know you aren't competitive . . . well, at least not any more than anyone else."

"You want to hear something frustrating? Today I found out that, despite all my work, I'm in a three-way dead heat for valedictorian."

"That's hard to believe." Mom stopped rinsing pasta. "How did you feel about that?"

"Well, I'm glad I'm in the running, but I'm discouraged that academics are not going to do it."

"What *is* going to do it?"

"The panel decided to look at our record of volunteer work." Olivia added the cheese and croutons. "I don't know if I can come up with a single thing, except for maybe a few church things." She began tossing the salad again. "I'm going to have to find myself a volunteer gig on top of everything else."

"Don't take it out on the salad, honey." The smell of garlic brought Sherman and Dad into the kitchen in time to take the plates Mom filled. "Why not talk to Diane when you go to youth group on Sunday? She knows the volunteer climate. I'll bet she can plug you in somewhere."

After asking a blessing on the food, the four of them talked over their day. Olivia listened, but she couldn't stop worrying about her schedule. *"Do not be anxious about anything."* The verse popped into her mind. *Good advice. The situation is what it is. I just need to take it one step at a time.*

Puggles nosed the side of her leg under the table, and she slid her hand down with a small piece of garlic bread. *Like Mom won't notice the dog's breath. Oh, well.* A person could get away with precious little in the O'Donnell household.

But Mom was right. Diane knew about all the agencies using volunteers.

When the dishes were done, Olivia took out her day planner and turned to Sunday to pencil in another reminder: "Explore volunteer opportunities with Diane Javier." There. A plan.

3

Hey, Olivia. How's your senior year shaping up?" Diane slid the spatula under a brownie and put it onto a paper plate. Besides being one of the coolest adults in the church, Diane was the wife of Pastor Joe, their youth minister.

"Yum. Inside brownies—my favorite. Thank you." Olivia and Diane were kindred spirits in so many things. Only Diane would remember that Olivia preferred gooey brownies. Jane liked the drier outside-edge brownies. "It's hard to believe I'm a senior already."

Olivia licked the brownie goo off her finger. "Things are OK."

"Just OK? How's the quest for the top spot going?"

"Now there's the rub." Olivia poured a glass of milk. Most of the kids who stayed after youth group had already wolfed down their snack and hit the foosball table or congregated around Joe. Jane and some of the others were working on a fund-raising idea with him. She heard an enthusiastic, thoroughly British-sounding "fantastic" from Jane.

"Do you have time to talk, Diane? I'll help with cleanup afterward."

"Sure. It doesn't need to be super private, does it?"

"No. I just need some advice."

Diane poured a glass of milk to go with her brownie, and they found a quiet corner.

"OK, shoot. What's happening with your quest for the gold?" Diane always cut right to the quick.

"I figured with the AP classes I took last year, I had it clinched; but this week I get to school and find out I'm in a three-way tie."

"Will they have co-valedictorians?"

"I don't think so. They announced that the graduation panel plans to look past academics and factor in each person's volunteer efforts." Olivia put her brownie down on the chair next to her. "Volunteerism has never been my thing."

"Hmmm. That's an interesting wrinkle, isn't it?"

"It's not fair." Olivia hated hearing the whine in her voice. "I mean, they changed the rules at the eleventh hour."

"Why do you say you are not a volunteer type?" Diane finished eating her brownie and set the empty

plate on the floor. She leaned forward and put her fore-
arms on her knees—prepared to listen.

Olivia sighed. *How to put it in words?* It was not that
she was a selfish person; she did care about others,
but— "I don't know. It's just that I'm all about grades."
That did sound selfish. "I mean, there's not time for
everything, and a person has to pick and choose, right?"

"I agree. There's never enough time." Diane waited
for Olivia to go on.

"I guess I'm feeling frustrated. Had I known, I would
have managed to work something in over my four
years." She drew a deep breath. "As it stands now, I'll
have to turn myself inside out to make a big enough
splash to be noticed."

"So what are you considering?"

"I don't know. That's why I wanted to talk to
you. You know so much about the helping-type
organizations."

"What do you like to do?"

"Read. Be with my friends. Watch *Changing Faces*
with Jane. Eat pizza."

Diane laughed. "You forgot to mention that you like
to come to youth group!"

"Oops."

"Just kidding—the friends and pizza are all part of
youth group, right?"

"Good save, Diane." Olivia laughed. Diane could always tease you into laughter. "I'm trying to work on my
priorities." She took out her day planner.

"Ah, the famous O'Donnell day planner. It sports a
longer to-do list than any planner I've ever seen."

"But it keeps me on task!"

"Look at this list. What a kick, Olivia. You've already

crossed out 'do not overschedule,' and it's only one week into the year." Diane laughed out loud.

"Sadly, it's the story of my life. Poor thing. It has more pencil scratchings and erasures than any day planner should ever have to endure."

"Back to your dilemma. You are committed to putting in some volunteer hours, right?"

"I have to."

"I won't argue with you on that point, though there are other options."

"Other options?"

"Have you considered being satisfied with salutatorian?"

Olivia gave Diane a look that would have withered a less stalwart mentor.

"OK . . . so what jobs would you hate?"

"I don't really like taking care of people physically. Wait—that sounds terrible. What I mean is that anything having to do with hospitals and caregiving makes me sweat bullets."

"Hmmm. Give me some other things that you definitely would *not* like."

"Honestly? I don't have a lot of patience with the down-and-out. You know, like welfare-type people." Olivia paused. "That sounds bad. I just get impatient with people who do not try hard enough." Olivia looked at Diane. She was hunched over in her serious listening mode, saying little and nodding a lot. *How I wish I could be as good a listener and as good a friend as Diane.*

"So working with needy people is out?"

"You must think I'm awful. You work with the homeless, don't you?"

Diane laughed. "Olivia, I'm not judging you; I'm just trying to help you sort things out. Did you ever think that God might have wired you with those particular likes and dislikes?"

"You mean God may have given me the gift of the television makeover and withheld the gift of mercy?"

Diane grabbed Olivia's head and did that noogie thing on her hair. "You crazy girl. The fact that you and Jane love *Changing Faces* has more to do with relationship and fun than with makeover. Of course, the fact that you're uncomfortable with the sick and needy may be an indication that you do not have the gift of mercy." Diane was quiet for a minute, and they watched Jane twist a mean foosball lever. "One thing is for sure— God is not done with you yet."

"Good thing."

"I'm not that much older than you. . . ."

Olivia pretended to look up at her in disbelief. In truth, Diane was young and beautiful—it was obvious that Pastor Joe was still crazy about her, even after four years of marriage. She loved clothes and color. Everyone commented on the way she combined things. Not many working women could get away with wearing lime green and purple, but Diane did it with style and looked professional in it.

"You stop! Whether you believe it or not, I haven't lived all that long, but I've seen the Lord take me places I'd never think of venturing."

"Like me doing volunteer work?"

"Maybe."

"So, got any ideas, O Wise One?"

"Open your day planner and write: 'Make an appointment with Diane Javier at The Shelter of His Wing.'"

"But you work at a homeless shelter. Remember that mercy-less thing?"

"Have faith in me, Olivia, my buddy. I'm not a volunteer at the shelter—it's my career. I'm the publicist and public relations director. We are getting ready for our big benefit and I could use organizational help."

"OK, I'll call tomorrow and make an appointment." She paused. "Thanks."

"I'm not making any promises since I'll have to run it by the director, Mrs. Bailey, but I know I could use your skill."

✿   ✿   ✿

Olivia looked out the window of the bus as she thumbed through her day planner.

True to her word, Diane had met with Olivia and pushed through the paperwork required to offer her the volunteer position of assistant publicist.

Olivia turned to the planner page bookmarked Today. She read, Shelter: 3:30 P.M.–5:30 P.M. The volunteer shelter hours would be challenging. She'd be working two hours on Monday and Wednesday after school and man the office alone on Saturday from nine to noon.

What a schedule. This would be a year she'd not soon forget. She flipped to her revised schedule. Sunday: A.M. Church, P.M. Youth group. Monday: School, Shelter: 3:30 P.M.–5:30 P.M., 7:30 P.M. Piano lessons, Homework. Tuesday: School, Tennis practice, Watching *Changing Faces* w/Jane. Wednesday: School, Shelter: 3:30 P.M.–5:30 P.M., Choir. Thursday: School, Tennis Match. Friday: School, Free afternoon and evening! Saturday: Shelter: 9 A.M. to Noon. Afternoon, evening—free!

Free. That was probably wishful thinking. She hadn't even attempted to schedule homework time and piano practice, nor did her planner carry any mention of room cleaning and dinner—two nonnegotiables. Mom expected her to do the dinner dishes, keep her room clean, plus help out with other chores occasionally. And dinner was a command performance. Because of their busy schedules, Mom and Dad insisted that everyone show up at six o'clock for dinner every night. It practically took an act of Congress to get a dinner release.

The nice thing about The Shelter of His Wing was that it was near the BART station in Hayward, so Olivia could walk to the BART station after school and be at the center in about a half hour. Good thing, since her parents didn't agree that a car was practically a necessity in high school. *Jane has no idea how lucky she is.*

There were no signs on the shelter building. Diane had said that was for safety reasons since the shelter catered to women and children. Some had escaped violent situations. When the bus pulled up at the building, Olivia got off along with another girl. She looked vaguely familiar—pretty with long dark brown hair and nearly black eyes. Did she attend Bay Vista?

"Hi, Olivia. Hi, Maria Elena." Diane met them at the door, answering their buzzer. "Did you two meet?"

"No." Olivia held out her hand to Maria Elena. "I'm Olivia. Do you volunteer here?"

The girl shook her head. "No, I'm staying here with my mother and little brother."

"Oh." Olivia could think of nothing else to say. *Stupid, stupid, stupid. This is why you're not fit for volunteer work.*

"Olivia is going to help me get ready for our benefit. Maria Elena, if you have any extra time, I could sure use your art skills, as well as your translation skills." Diane turned to Olivia. "Maria Elena not only speaks both English and Spanish, but she has a knack for phrasing things perfectly in either language."

"Wow." Olivia tripped all over her tongue in one language.

"I want to reach out to potential Latino benefactors with our promotional outreach as well as to the other people in our community."

"I'll ask my mother, Mrs. Javier."

"Call me Diane. Olivia does."

Maria Elena smiled a half smile. Olivia guessed that she'd rather use the more formal address.

"Do you always go by both names?" Olivia asked.

"Usually, but my mother calls me *mi hija*."

It sounded like *me-haw* to Olivia. "That means 'my daughter,' right?"

"Yes." Maria Elena was a girl of few words.

"Can I call you Mia? Maria Elena seems so long."

Diane laughed. "It doesn't take Olivia long to come up with a nickname, does it?"

"I like Mia." Maria Elena seemed in a hurry to go. "I need to check in with my mother. She worries about me riding the bus."

"Nice meeting you, Mia." Olivia could see that she had somehow made Maria Elena uncomfortable.

"Bye, Olivia. Bye, Mrs. . . . Diane."

When she disappeared down a corridor, Olivia turned to Diane. "Did I say something to make her uneasy?"

"No. Maria Elena is probably uncomfortable with

someone from school finding out she lives in a shelter. That, and the fact that her whole life's been turned upside down."

"I can already see that I'm no good at this. I don't think I have a sensitive bone in my whole body." Had she made a poor choice for her volunteer work? Shouldn't she have tutored some of the church kids in reading or math instead?

"Maybe God's just planning to stretch you a little bit. We talk about wanting God to rock our world, but then we make sure not to move a single inch out of our comfort zones."

Olivia licked her index finger and sketched a number one in the air. "Your point, O Wise One." Olivia laughed. "OK, stretch away."

"C'mon, smart aleck. Let me give you the nickel tour. First, the gym."

"Gym?"

"Well, it's really a multipurpose room, but we try to have lots of physical activities for the kids who live here. They usually land here in the middle of a crisis, and we find that nothing helps relieve stress like working muscles."

"You don't mind if I take a few notes, do you? I want to be able to retain everything you tell me." Olivia pulled out her day planner.

"You and your planner." Diane laughed.

They heard the reverberating sound of a basketball on a gym floor as soon as they entered the building housing the gym. Screams of kids, the squeak of tennis shoes, and the begging cries of "throw it here, throw it here" were punctuated by the blast of a whistle.

Olivia continued writing as they walked, trying to

catch all that Diane had said earlier. As Diane pushed open the door into the gym, Olivia moved through without looking up.

"You said they usually come directly out of crisis?" Olivia wanted to get it right.

"Yes." Diane stopped, and Olivia nearly bumped into her. "OK, this is the gym, and this is our after-school activity program."

"After-school activity program," Olivia repeated as she wrote. As she looked up, she realized that the room had quieted.

There stood Carter Wylie, whistle in mouth, surrounded by a group of boys—all looking directly at her.

"Guys, this is my new assistant, Olivia O'Donnell." Diane put her arm on Olivia's shoulder.

Carter tipped an imaginary hat at her, then blew the whistle to resume play.

What an idiot I must've seemed. Walking head down into the middle of their game. Without saying a word, Olivia slipped back out the door before anyone could see her flaming cheeks.

"Olivia?"

"Nice gym, Diane." She felt like groaning out loud. Carter—the one guy she'd really noticed. As Jane had said, he was a hottie. *Well, there's no question now. I'll be leaving him to the likes of Aubrey after that faux pas.* "Let's finish the tour. I want to help you, not keep you away from your desk."

Olivia wondered if Carter lived here at the shelter as well. Not that it mattered. After that embarrassing moment, she'd do her best to make sure their paths never crossed. Too bad he had those gorgeous crinkles at the corners of his mouth when he smiled.

4

Hurry, Jane. It's about to start."

"Fantastic. They're doing a college girl today. Brilliant! I love it when they do people our age."

"Like they'd ever do a high school student." Olivia threw a pillow at Jane's head.

"College is close enough." Jane retaliated with the pillow, whapping Olivia over the side of the head a couple of times. "Truce. I don't want to miss this."

"I notice you didn't call truce until you delivered the last blow." Olivia pushed the sleeping Puggles farther under the coffee table. Not that he'd wake. When he slept, nothing bothered him.

The commercials over, Kinni McKay, the host of *Changing Faces*, gave the intro. "Her friends say she is more books than looks; more academics than aesthetics; more study than party. We agree. Take a look at these snaps sent in by her friends."

"Yikes, she dresses like you, O." Jane didn't take her eyes from the screen.

"No fair. I usually try to iron a cotton blouse before I wear it—don't I?"

Jane turned, lowered her head in that no-nonsense way, and gave Olivia a silent look.

"OK, not if it's a test day, but—"

"In your defense, let me state, for the record, that you would never wear sweatpants to class."

"Right."

"Flannel pajama bottoms, maybe, but never sweatpants."

"You're too cruel. Watch the TV and stop picking on me."

Just then Kinni McKay brought out the guest. "Meet Jennifer, a mild-mannered coed who is about to get the makeover of her life."

The B-roll began, showing Jennifer in her apartment, at classes, and leading a group of grade school kids around a science museum.

"You're a busy girl, Jenn," Kinni said when the mini-documentary of her life ended. "Your friends think that you are in need of a makeover to get you ready for graduation and your job hunt. What do you think?"

"I think I'm going to kill my friends."

"Even when you see this check for three thousand

dollars for new clothes?" Kinni, still facing the camera, waved a check in front of her.

"Well, maybe not." The girl laughed. "But that photo in sweats cannot be easily forgiven."

"So, Jenn, are you ready to . . . change faces?" Kinni's voice dropped down into television-announcer mode on those last two words, and the music faded in.

From there, the show moved to the segment where the show's staff looked at her wardrobe and explained why the pieces didn't work and what could be substituted. This was always done with humor.

"Kinni's going easy on her," Jane said when the host picked up the shapeless sweatpants and tossed them. "I would have made her squirm."

"I bet those sweatpants have aced many a cellular microbiology midterm."

Jane rolled her eyes. "It's not all about grades, y'know."

"It's not?" Olivia gave her innocent smile and batted her eyelashes. Good thing she had such long eyelashes since she rarely got a chance to put mascara on them.

With the *Changing Faces* "before" part out of the way, the real fun began. First came the shopping spree, when the guest began by shopping on her own. She kept getting sidetracked by sweats and slouchy styles until Kinni joined her to guide her to styles that would flatter her shape but still work for her lifestyle. They even ended up with a couple of suits and blazers for the career that would follow graduation. After that segment, the scene faded as the music announced time for a commercial break.

Jane jumped up. Every break in the show offered an opportunity for Jane and Olivia to either visit or get up and hit the kitchen. "Boy, am I glad you don't have a car, so we always watch the show here at your house," Jane said.

"You're glad I don't have a car?" Olivia stopped rummaging in the pantry.

"No, no. I don't mean that—what I mean is that if we came to my house to watch *Changing Faces*, the fridge would have nothing but leftovers that look like specimen dishes for biology class. My mother hates grocery shopping, and I—"

"Well, I'm glad my mom always keeps the pantry and fridge stocked," Olivia said, cutting Jane off, "but I wish I had a car."

"I know." Jane found the container of fruit leather Olivia's mom had made over the summer. The chewy sweetness was exactly what Jane needed at the moment. She poured a half glass of cranberry juice and filled the rest with ginger ale.

"My life would be so much easier." Olivia took a bag of carrot snacks. Not that she was on a health food kick—she just thought they looked good. "Do you know how hard it is to get around efficiently when you have to bum rides and use public transportation?"

"Whoa. I didn't mean to get you started, O."

Olivia laughed. "OK. I know you've heard all this before, but why did I have to draw the parents who believe a car is something kids have to earn on their own?"

Jane grabbed her favorite drink. "Have you made any progress on your auto fund?"

"Not a penny. I was hoping to work in a part-time job, but with this volunteering thing I'll be walking till I'm thirty."

"Oh, yeah, I meant to ask you—how did that go? The volunteer thing."

The music came on, signaling the end of the commercial break.

"Oops. The makeup and hair makeover is starting. I don't want to miss it. I'll tell you the whole humiliating story at the next commercial." Olivia flopped on the floor next to the coffee table.

"Oh, stop!" Jane shot up off the couch, talking to the television. "No. They are not taking her to Sephora for the makeover." She dramatically put her hands over her heart. "If I had a *Changing Faces* makeover at Sephora, I might as well die. Nothing else in life would compare."

Olivia laughed. Jane could be a drama queen.

The makeup artist mixed the face powders right on the spot, testing the color on Jenny's jawline. "With a young woman, we only apply a fine dusting to even out any blotchiness."

"Good thing," Jane said. "Those are some full-blown zits on her forehead."

"I'd hate to have a camera zoom in on my freshly scrubbed skin," Olivia admitted.

"A light dusting of blush across her cheekbones is all that's needed to give her a glow—a look of translucence." The camera angle changed as the makeup artist applied wax to the guest's eyebrow area. "We want to shape Jenn's eyebrows, but we will avoid taking too much off. Too many young women overpluck these days and miss out on a dramatic frame for their eyes." *Rip!* "See how removing the stray hairs and shaping the under brow opens up Jenn's eyes?"

"Ouch! That's easy for her to say." Olivia was still wincing. "Look at the tears in that poor girl's eyes."

"My grandma used to say, 'It hurts to be beautiful.'" Jane finished the last of her drink and set the glass down on the table.

The camera cut to the eye makeup segment. "Because Jenn's eyes are big already, we'll just put a dusky eye shadow across her lid. Next we'll give her a smudge of liner on top and bottom—subtle, to let her natural beauty show." Another camera angle change. "Her well-shaped lips need nothing more than a shimmer of rosy gloss. Take a look in the mirror, Jennifer."

The girl looked in the mirror, as the screen split between the before-shot and the after-shot.

"Makeup, applied with a light hand, only enhances her beauty." The makeup artist smiled at the image in the mirror. The camera faded and the show went to commercial.

"That does look amazing, doesn't it?" Jane turned and looked at Olivia. "That would work for you since your eyes are so big."

"Maybe. I may try it if I ever find time."

"That reminds me—how did the volunteer thing go?" Jane asked.

"Well, I got the job, but—"

"Was there any doubt?"

"Oh, yes. It may be a volunteer position, but Diane says they are very careful in choosing staff. I guess it's important for staff to be careful with the safety stuff."

"What do you mean, 'safety stuff'?" Jane untucked her feet and leaned forward. "Is it dangerous?"

"I guess it could be. They try to keep the location a secret because some women are escaping from abusive situations. Husbands or boyfriends could become violent in trying to get them back."

"It doesn't sound like much fun." Jane threw a pillow on the floor and joined Olivia. "This is where Diane works?"

"Yep. Though she doesn't work directly with the people. She does the PR stuff and the fund-raising."

"What will you do?"

"I'm going to try to help her organize things. Everyone there has way more work than they can handle, and the whole thing runs on a shoestring."

"A shoestring?"

"You know—no money." She rubbed her thumbs against her fingers. "I guess it's a challenge for them to house and feed all the residents. Diane says they turn away families every week."

"How awful. Poor Diane."

"I know. I hope I can help her, but I don't know how I'm ever going to work all this in." She reached over and patted her already-bulging day planner. It never left her side.

As the *Changing Faces* logo flashed, the friends settled in for the end of the show. A hairstylist cut the girl's hair, taking off some of the weight and working with the natural wave. The before and after screen showed a more polished, more shaped Jennifer before it cut to yet another commercial.

"So what was the embarrassing part you mentioned earlier?"

Olivia flopped onto her back and covered her eyes with her arm. "I totally humiliated myself. I was so intent on taking notes during my orientation that I walked right into the middle of a basketball game."

"Was it a serious game?"

"Oh, I don't know if it was a game or a practice or what." She sighed, dragging the air in through her nostrils. "That's not the bad part. You know that new guy in first period?"

"Carter?"

"Yes. Carter of the dark brown hair, big blue eyes, and gorgeous smile."

"Uh-oh. You know Aubrey's got her eye on that one. Tall, dark, and handsome."

Olivia laughed. "Give me a break! Aubrey's got her eye on every good-looking guy."

"Tell me the rest. Let's not get off on Aubrey when you've got info to dish."

"Right. Besides, I'm totally ignoring Aubrey this year."

Jane laughed. "Right."

"Anyway, as I stumbled onto the court looking like a dork, there stands Carter with a whistle in his mouth, having to halt the play to keep me from getting trampled."

"What was he doing there?"

"I have no idea. I was so mortified that I forgot to ask Diane. I don't know if he works there or if he lives there." Olivia sat up. "I already made a mistaken assumption with Maria Elena, a girl who goes to Bay Vista. I got off BART with her, and when I saw her at the center, I asked if she worked there."

"And?"

"She hesitated—obviously hating to say that she lives there at the center. I could tell it bothered her to admit it to someone from school."

"So you think Carter may live there?"

"I have no idea. I do know he runs the sports program there." Olivia rubbed a spot on the coffee table. "I'm so no good when it comes to stuff like this. I seem to fall all over myself and do the wrong thing. I think I'm missing the compassionate gene."

"Yikes! Don't say that. Remember what Pastor Joe said last Sunday night?" Jane looked up and saw the *Changing Faces* screen once more. "Wait. Here's the reveal."

The show resumed with what they called the "reveal." Jennifer modeled her new clothes, makeup, and hairstyle for Kinni while an offscreen announcer gave the commentary—almost like a fashion show. Then they cut to the final segment—Jennifer back in her own environment. She walked into a campus party with her new look to the amazed comments of family and friends.

"That was too cool." Jane stretched. "What were we talking about?"

"You mentioned Pastor Joe's message." Olivia thought back to his talk. She usually listened carefully. Pastor Joe's no-nonsense approach to God always made so much sense. He and Diane were among her favorite people. "Remind me."

"He said that when an area of shortcoming shows up in our spiritual walk, it's often God tapping us on the shoulder—letting us know what our next challenge will be."

"I remember. He said that it's often the beginning of a whole new journey." Puggles came up and gave Olivia a wet puppy kiss. "Yuck, Puggles. Who woke you up?"

"He's probably telling you that if you don't let him out you'll end up with puddles by Puggles."

Olivia jumped up to let the dog run out into the backyard. Jane was right. Olivia had thought a lot about her lack of compassion ever since the volunteer thing came up. Could God really be challenging her in this area? But then why were all her talents in a different direction?

Jane stood up and brought her glass into the kitchen. "I probably should head home. I thought homework during our senior year was supposed to be lighter."

"That's the big lie."

Jane changed the subject. "Don't worry about Carter. I'm sure he saw you with your nose in your notes and was bowled over by your commitment."

"Good try, Jane, but I looked like an idiot."

"I'll try to find out where he lives."

"Be careful. I don't want you to put him on the spot."

"I'll get it out of Aubrey. By now she not only knows his digits, she probably knows his social security number and his bank balance."

"That's what I'm afraid of."

"OK, O. We need to talk. Are you crushing here?"

"Crushing?"

"You know! Have you got a thing for him?"

"Jane! Go home." Olivia narrowed her eyes and picked up the nearest weapon—a purple chenille fringed pillow. "You know I'm all about keeping my eye on the prize. No guy stuff for me."

"OK. I'm out of here. I know when I'm not welcome." Jane flipped her hair, taking long dramatic strides to the door, doing her very best Jean Harlow impersonation. "I have just one question, dahling."

Olivia guessed what was coming.

"What if the prize on which you've fixed your eye turns out to be one Carter Wylie?" Jane ducked out of the door before Olivia could throw another pillow at her head.

Carter indeed, thought Olivia. Like she could fit him into her planner.

"Olivia." Diane looked up from a pile of file folders on her desk. "Am I ever glad to see you."

Good thing someone's glad to see me. On the way into Diane's office, Olivia had tripped over two boys playing cars on the floor. Just when she picked herself up, another boy came running by and slammed into her backpack.

"Ouch." The boy rubbed his head. "Whatcha got in there? Bricks?"

"Isn't it customary to say 'excuse me' when you run into someone?" Olivia didn't wait for an answer. It was bad enough that she didn't even have time to go home and drop off her books before catching BART to come to the center, but the day had gone from bad to worse. Some kids she knew held after-school jobs that actually paid money. They worked at trendy clothing stores or coffee shops where they'd meet interesting people.

She looked around the reception area. Utter confusion. The desk was empty. Two girls sat underneath playing with a couple of frazzled-looking Barbies. Besides the boys playing cars, bigger boys zigzagged through the room on their way to the gym.

Mia came through, giving a half wave to Olivia. "Did you kids get your snacks in the kitchen?"

"Yuck," said one of the car-playing boys. "They only got apples or raisins. I like candy."

Olivia looked at him and shook her head as she stepped over the mess to make her way to Diane's office. *Boys!* She was glad Tank was out of grammar school.

"Don't you even say hi?"

She turned around. How had she missed seeing Carter sitting on the steps to the sleeping quarters?

"Hi, Carter." She wondered how long he'd been watching her. "I'm doing my best to step over this chaos and avoid the riffraff on my way to the offices."

"Whoa. Sounds like someone has a chip on her shoulder. What do you think, Markie?"

One of the boys stopped ramming his car across the floor and looked up. "Nope. Those are backpack straps. Don't see no chip." He took his car and crashed it into the one in his friend's hand.

"I've got a job to do." Olivia couldn't believe he sat

there judging her. If only he weren't so good-looking as he did it.

"So your job is more important than giving a friendly word or a smile to these guys?" Carter's grin took some of the sting out of the words.

Olivia could see that he was trying to gently nudge her. "You're probably right, but I'm all about organization, not kids. That's why I'm heading to the office and not to the playroom."

"All right, Chip, but we're going to be watching you, aren't we, kids?"

Olivia sighed. *Why me? What am I doing here?*

That's why it was nice to see Diane's face light up as she walked into the office.

"You look like you've had a rough day." Diane pulled out a chair. "Drop your pack and tell Auntie Diane. It's time for a break, anyway."

Olivia dropped her backpack. "I had to run the gauntlet in the entryway."

"There's not enough room in the playroom, and the bigger kids use the gym in the afternoon." Diane popped open a can of cranapple juice and poured half into a paper cup. "Can or cup?"

"Can. Thanks." She sank into a chair. "How long has Carter lived here?"

"Carter?"

"Carter Wylie. The guy who does gym with the kids."

Diane laughed. "Carter doesn't live here." She put her feet up on a box of files. "I don't mean to laugh— there's nothing funny about living here, but Carter's dad made his money in computer networking. Internet switches or something. He sold his company to one of the Silicon Valley biggies and moved over to this side of the bay."

Olivia shook her head. "His dad?"

"He's on our board of directors here at The Shelter of His Wing. If it weren't for him—"

"So if Carter is a rich Silicon Valley kid, what in the world is he doing here?" Olivia knew that most of the families who'd made their fortune in the computer industry sent their kids to prep schools and lived in Mission Hills.

"Carter's as dedicated to the center as his dad. His mom died when he was still in preschool. He's a committed Christian, you know." Diane put her cup into the trash.

"I'm beginning to see that I know very little. Carter just lectured me."

"Carter? He's so easygoing. What in the world did you do?"

"When I came in, all I wanted to do was make my way to your office and dump my load. I tripped over two boys. When another collided with me, I simply asked him why he didn't excuse himself."

"Doesn't sound so bad to me."

"Carter implied that I had no right to correct him when I had neither greeted him, smiled at him, or acknowledged him." Olivia tried to work up an indignant snort, but as she heard her words, she knew Carter had a point. "I told you I was no good with mercy."

The door opened behind her.

"I seem to have no patience for the down-and-out. I don't even know how people get to this place in their lives." She looked at Diane's face, which was focused now on someone behind her.

"Hello, Maria Elena. Did you come to help Olivia work on organizing me?"

"N–no." Her voice barely gave sound to her words. "*No.* I mean, I need to do other things."

Olivia turned around and saw the stricken look on Mia's face. She knew Maria Elena had heard her stupid wail.

"Please stay, Mia. I didn't mean—"

"No. I must . . . I must do something." She backed out of the door, but not before the tears filled the bottom lids of her eyes.

"Oh, Diane. I didn't mean for her to hear that. In fact, I don't know why I even said it. When I think about the down-and-out, I don't think about people with faces I know." Olivia laid her head on the desk. "How could I be so cold?"

"I should have managed to interrupt you. When Maria Elena thinks about it, she'll know you were speaking theoretically and that you don't mean it personally." Diane stood up and came over to Olivia, putting a hand on each side of her face. "Don't worry. I'll speak to her. Maria Elena's very wise and very forgiving."

"I'm not cut out for this kind of thing, Diane. Can't you see?"

"I see just the opposite. You've got a ways to go, but you are just what the doctor ordered for me." Diane swept her hand in an arc, indicating the room. "I need help."

Olivia put her can in the box overflowing with empty cans and stood up. "All right. I can't undo the mess I just made—at least not right now—so why don't you tell me what needs doing here?"

Diane showed her the file cabinets and the stacks of files on the desk and on the floor. "I'm in the middle of trying to clean out the file cabinets. It's time to start fresh on this year's benefit."

"Benefit?"

"We have one big fund-raiser each year. As the publicity director, I spend much of the year building toward that event. Our job is to plan the event, to publicize it, and to fill it with potential donors."

Olivia took out her planner and opened it to the back where she kept blank sheets. "Let me take some notes."

"Why does that not surprise me?" Diane laughed. "You, my friend, are exactly what I need."

Olivia didn't answer. She still had a hollow feeling in the pit of her stomach.

"How late are you staying?"

"Dad's going to pick me up on his way home from work, so it's probably going to be about five forty-five."

"I leave today at five, but there's plenty to do." Diane picked up a stack of files. "Take all these folders from last year's event and put them into these cardboard file storage boxes."

"Shall I type labels for the new files as I box them?" Olivia figured it would be an easy way to develop the new system since there was a separate label maker right on her table.

"See. That's why I need you." Diane cleared her desk onto Olivia's table. "I keep thinking of Paul's greeting to the Philippians, 'I thank my God every time I remember you. . . .'"

Diane went to work at her desk, and Olivia at her table.

"I've got to get going." Diane stood up. Taking her jacket off the back of her chair, she slipped it on and reached under her desk for her purse. "Will you be OK?"

"Of course. There's plenty of work to keep me busy."

Diane laughed as she walked out the door. "Truer words were never spoken."

Olivia kept at it until a knock on the door interrupted her.

"Hi, Chip. Can I come in?" Carter walked in and perched on the edge of her table.

"Sure. Besides, aren't you already in?"

"I've heard that it's pretty hard to get penciled in on your schedule." Though his words sounded like kidding, he didn't smile.

"You must have talked to my longtime friend, Aubrey." *Crud! Why did I respond with a snipe at Aubrey? You're ignoring her, remember?*

"And others."

Olivia could tell he was stalling. She didn't know him well, but this didn't seem like him. "You're here, so shoot."

"Diane tells me you're a straightforward person."

Olivia didn't say anything. Why was he talking about her to Diane? She waited.

"I'll be straight with you. I think you need to talk to Maria Elena."

"Mia?"

"I caught up with her as she ran out of this room. I couldn't pry out the reason for the tears, but I do know that she's devastated."

Olivia knew he was right. "What did she say?"

"She said she hated her life. Hated living here. Hated her stepfather for making them have to run to safety—"

Olivia put up her hand. "Don't say any more. Please." She shook her head. "Mia walked in on me spewing garbage about the down-and-out. I didn't mean her."

"No wonder."

"I told Diane I'm no good at this. I told her when we first talked." Olivia could hear the defensiveness in her voice. "I mean, I know I'm at fault here, but—"

"Whoa, Chip." Carter shook his head and smiled. "I didn't mean to come in and accuse you. I just knew you'd want to make things right with Maria Elena."

"I do. It's just that I'm like a steamroller when it comes to sensitive situations." She sighed. "I told Diane that I'm totally missing the gift of mercy."

Carter laughed. "You are something else."

"I don't think it's funny."

"But just because we don't have a 'gift' in a certain area"—he made quote marks in the air—"doesn't mean the Lord doesn't expect us to work on that area." Carter smiled at her—that beautiful smile. "You are so good at organizing, but don't miss the real treasure—the people."

"Oh, please don't give me the 'God is stretching you' speech."

Carter laughed. "Sounds like I don't need to."

"I'm going to talk to Mia." *And then I'm going to talk to Diane and resign.* "I'm not suited for this job, but I do want to make things right with Mia."

"I knew you would, whether or not I said anything to you."

56

"Then why'd you come in?"

"Maybe I just wanted to talk to you." Carter hopped off the desk and left.

Olivia sat looking at the door.

Sephora

6

How long has it been since we planned a day together?" Olivia stretched her arms up toward the roof of Jane's car.

"Too long, that's for sure, but trying to squeeze into your schedule has been near impossible."

"Oh, no. Please don't start. I'm getting it from everyone." Olivia looked out the window. She and Jane had wanted to visit Sephora ever since they saw it on a *Changing Faces* episode. They'd finally decided on today. "Is this ever the perfect day for our pilgrimage!"

"I love fall. Look at the leaves. They're brilliant. Lit-rally fantastic." Jane lapsed into her faux-Brit accent.

It was no exaggeration for once. The canyon vibrated with color. "I'm so glad we have to drive through Niles Canyon to get to Stoneridge." Olivia looked down at the creek. The water churned up a bubbly froth as it tumbled over the rocks. The trees nearest the water sported the most dazzling color. With the sun shining through the leaves, the air practically vibrated with yel-lows and oranges. "People think you have to go to New England to see fall color. Wouldn't they be surprised to see our pockets of color here in California?"

"I can hardly believe we are finally doing this." Jane hit the dashboard with the palm of her hand to empha-size her disbelief.

"Will you stop? You make it sound like spending the day with me is a rarity." Olivia smiled. "We used to spend so much time together that my dad threatened to claim you on his income tax."

Jane didn't laugh. "The key phrase is 'used to spend so much time together.'"

"Jane, you know what my life is like. I'm going crazy with—"

"You're right. I know what your life is like." Jane paused as she navigated the tight turn on the narrow bridge over the creek. "Do you know what my life is like?"

"What do you mean?" *This is supposed to be a day to enjoy each other—to reconnect. We never fight. What is this about?*

"I mean that you have no idea what's going on in my life."

Olivia looked puzzled.

"Do you know which classes I love this year? Do you know about the sophomore who is following me around like a puppy? Do you know what movies are on my Christmas list? Do you know what writing project I'll have to spend Thanksgiving break doing?"

Olivia didn't answer. It seemed more like an accusation than an invitation to conversation.

"For the record, it's choir, Jonathan Arnold, *Meet Me in St. Louis* with Judy Garland, *Roman Holiday*, and college essays."

"I guess it's a little late to ask what's up with you." Olivia didn't quite know how to respond. As they rounded a curve, fallen leaves skittered across the road like dancing confetti.

Jane smiled a little sheepishly. "I didn't mean to dump all this on you. I guess I've been storing up a touch of resentment, and I guess it sort of came spewing forth and—"

"Don't you be apologizing, Jane. You were right to bring it up. You were right on every point. I'm so over-scheduled I'm not even being a good friend."

"We'll let today change all that, 'kay?" Jane gave her a light punch on her arm. "Today is the first day of the rest of our lives."

Olivia groaned out loud. "Got any more worn-out pronouncements to interrupt my heartfelt apology?"

Jane laughed. "You're right. I need my proper apology. Then, and only then, will I pepper you with gag-worthy sentiments."

Olivia put her hand over heart in mock seriousness. "Will you forgive me for not keeping up with everything in your life? Will you forgive me for not knowing what TV shows you watched last night and what deodorant currently tops your hit parade? Will you forgive me for not helping you wash your car and clean your room? Will you—?"

"OK, enough already. This could go on forever, and you still would only skim the surface." Jane laughed, her sense of humor firmly back in place. "I graciously offer forgiveness for all the unintentional slights you've perpetrated on our friendship in your quest to be all that you can be."

"How you managed to include the army's slogan into your response is nothing short of amazing. If it weren't for clichés today, you'd barely have anything to say." *Thank goodness the tense conversation seems over and the familiar teasing fun is back.*

"Besides, love means never having to say you're sorry." Jane looked straight ahead as she slowed up for the four-way stop.

"That was the worst pronouncement you've offered to date. Besides, it's not true. When we love someone, we ask forgiveness." Olivia put her hand on Jane's arm as soon as the car stopped. "I may tease you, but you were right on all counts. You are my best friend, and I've ignored you badly. Thank you for putting up with me."

The car behind them honked.

"Oops. Better drive." Jane turned left toward Pleasanton. "Apology accepted. I know how busy life is for you. I just miss you. I've been guilty of piling up hurts for a while. Friends don't do that, y'know."

"Well, today will make up for all that. I can't wait to do this Sephora thing. It's almost like getting to be on *Changing Faces*," Olivia said.

"I know. I hope they'll have two makeover spots open so we can have our faces done at the same time."

It was only ten more minutes until they pulled into the huge mall parking lot. Olivia still mulled over the conversation with Jane. When she got home, she planned to pencil Jane in on her list of goals. No. She'd write Jane's name in ink. *I need to make friendship a priority.* As they walked into the mall, a question came to mind: *How many top priorities can one person have?*

"C'mon." Jane grabbed Olivia's hand. "It's over here."

"You're not in a hurry or anything, are you?"

"This is so exciting. I love this store!" Jane slowed her pace. "OK, I'll slow down so we'll look as if we do this every day. I've only got so much money, so I can't decide if I should go with the shimmery evening-type look or be practical and get stuff for a day look. Of course, I could—"

"You could wait until we get into the store and then decide." The old Jane was back—talking up a storm. Olivia knew they'd passed the rough spot.

Jane continued as if Olivia had not interrupted. "I know I should concentrate on skin care, but that's the most expensive and it doesn't really show—"

"Jane!" Olivia stopped, causing her friend to jerk to a stop as well. "You are obsessing."

"How can you stay so calm? We've talked about this forever." Jane took a deep breath. "OK, I've visibly calmed myself. See, I'm calm. Let's go."

Everything was such fun with Jane. The cool, bored girls at Bay Vista were much admired, but Olivia knew they got old quick. *Give me a Jane Broga any day. The whole world seems to hum when Jane is around.* "Hey, look."

"What?"

"The Franklin Covey store." Olivia pointed across the walk. "Can you imagine? A whole store dedicated to organizational systems?" Olivia did the mental calculations. Could she afford to divide her little stash of cash to buy something at Sephora and still have money left for some new elements for her day planner?

"Don't you even think about it, Olivia O'Donnell. If you so much as step one foot into that store, me and my Jetta will leave you stranded." Jane pulled her toward Sephora. "You, my friend, do not need another organizer. You need a healthy dose of disorganization. When's the last time you kicked back?"

"Don't start on me, missy." Olivia used her mock-mother voice. "What do you think I'm doing right now?"

"Oh, look." Jane was off again. "A kiosk filled with bracelet charms. I so want to get one of these. I think I'm the only one who hasn't started a bracelet yet."

"That reminds me. Do you know what someone in fifth period told me?"

"What?"

"You know those three almost-full bracelets Aubrey wears?"

"Yeah?" Jane sounded wary.

"All filled with alphabet letter charms?"

"Yeah? I thought you made a pledge to ignore Aubrey this year."

"Wait, though. This is too good," Olivia said. "Each charm represents the first initial of a guy's name. I'm not kidding. You know how I've always said she 'trophy' dates?" Olivia sketched quote marks in the air. "Well, I wasn't so far off the mark. Those charms represent the 'trophies' she's collected over her high school years— one charm for each guy."

Jane didn't say anything.

"Is that cheesy or what?" Olivia waited for Jane to add some of her famous acerbic remarks. But Jane seemed uncomfortable. "What's the matter? Don't you think that's wild?"

"Aubrey's not so bad." Jane turned from the kiosk.

Olivia stood rooted to the spot. "Wait a minute, Jane. What is up?" OK, she knew she was wrong for gossiping about Aubrey—especially in light of the goal to totally ignore her and end the Aubrey competition thing this year—but having a bracelet sporting a string of conquests was too quirky a detail not to enjoy.

"Nothing's up." Jane stopped and plopped down on a bench. "It's just that I've gotten to know Aubrey better this year, and she's not like we thought she was—not entirely." Jane seemed evasive.

"How have you gotten to know her better?" Olivia could hardly believe Jane was defending Aubrey.

"Well, you've been so busy this year, I've hardly seen you." Jane didn't look up.

Olivia sat down. "I know. We already had this discussion once today. Remember?"

"Well, when Aubrey found out how much time you were spending at the center, she invited me to come over and do homework with her on those days. She said she could see I was at loose ends."

"You've been going there a couple times a week?" *Stop it, Olivia. Jane has to have other friends as well.* She felt as if she'd been hit in the stomach. Just why did it have to be Aubrey—the one person who'd always had it in for her?

"I've really been helping Aubrey bring up her grades."

Olivia didn't know what to say.

"Plus, she invited me to her Halloween party with all her friends. You were at the center that day, remember?"

"I remember." Olivia knew she needed to get over this or she'd ruin their whole day. "I'm sorry I said anything about her bracelets, but I still think it's weird."

Jane seemed relieved. "I'm so glad I told you." She put her arm around Olivia. "We'll always be best friends, but I know you are totally tied up this year. I didn't want to go through my senior year without friends, and at first I hung with Aubrey to kind of spite you, but you were too busy to notice—" Jane ran out of breath but barely paused to get a fresh gulp. "After a while I sort of came to like Aubrey. She goes way out of her way to include me."

I'll bet she does.

"Her mom invited me to go with them to the city for shopping the day after Thanksgiving."

"That should be fun." *Looks like I might be the one to go through my senior year without friends.*

"I know." Jane let a breath out. "I'm so glad I told you, O. It's been making me feel like I've been disloyal, but . . ."

Olivia didn't know what to say. *Let it go, Olivia. You just gotta deal.* She changed the subject. "Let's get to Sephora before they sell out of everything."

"Right. Brilliant." Jane stood up. "One more thing and then we're done talking about Aubrey. She asked if she could start coming to our youth group. I couldn't very well say no."

"Oh." Olivia found herself short of words again. *Stop it. What's wrong with you? Don't you want Aubrey to share your faith? You can figure out a way to stay out of her way at youth group. Get over it!* She put a smile on her face. "That's good, Jane."

"Yeah. I was happy she was so interested after all the years she mocked our youth group." Jane started walking again, pointedly ignoring the charm kiosk. "C'mon, let's go."

☆   ☆   ☆

"You look brilliant, O." Jane clutched her glossy black-and-white Sephora bag as if it held the crown jewels. "Can you believe this tiny bag costs so much?"

Olivia held up her bag. "Yep. Mine is just as pricey." Olivia glanced one last time over at the Franklin Covey store as they walked toward the coffee shop. "I like what they did to my eyes, but I'm not sure about the rest. I feel a little made-up."

"It's just because you're not used to wearing makeup. If this was *Changing Faces,* Kinni would say, 'Makeup, artistically applied, only brings out the beauty that lies within,'" Jane said in a perfect Kinni McKay voice.

Olivia laughed. "That's *exactly* what she would say. I wonder if the guests worry their faces might crack if they smile too big at her comments?"

"You're hopeless. You'll never be a glam queen."

"Good thing. That makeover took almost an hour. I could never find a stray hour in my day to apply makeup."

"Speaking of that, how are things going at the center?"

"Honestly?"

"Always honestly." Jane opened the door of the coffee shop for her. "Wait until we get our double mocha frappuccinos. Then you need to tell sister Jane every-thing."

Once tucked into the corner of the coffee shop, Olivia put her cup on the table and leaned toward Jane. "It might cost me the valedictory address, but I'm going to quit as soon as I can talk to Diane."

"Why?" Jane put her cup down and folded her arms to listen.

"I am just no good at this."

"But you're the organization-meister."

"Oh, I'm doing a great job in the office—at least, according to Diane. I've got the files in order and all the tasks leading up to the spring benefit completely mapped out and scheduled." Olivia loved getting that out of the way. "I even updated Diane's media contacts and put them into a database so we could sort and re-trieve them a number of different ways."

"Doesn't sound very no-good to me."

"It's the people." Olivia paused. "I'm no good with the residents. I keep stumbling over kids, and I don't know what to say to the mothers I meet. I unintention-ally hurt Mia—"

"Mia?"

"You know, Maria Elena from school. She walked into the office when I was saying some stupid things. She overheard me."

"Was she upset?"

"According to Carter, very."

"I forgot Carter works there. Aubrey is always going on about Carter. You know he doesn't live there, don't you? I forgot to tell you I found that out."

"Thankfully, I discovered that before I made another dumb faux pas. How did you know?"

"Aubrey did some digging. Says his dad is one of the richest guys to come out of Silicon Valley."

"Yep. Carter's rich and cute—no wonder Aubrey's been digging." Olivia caught herself. "Yikes. Old habits die hard. Sorry for that, Jane."

"No prob. I know the troubles with Aubrey go back years, and I know she's not perfect." Jane took a napkin to carefully wipe foam off her Sephora-glossed lips. "What did Carter say?"

"It's actually what he didn't say that got to me. He's very encouraging—very nice."

"Nice. That sounds less than enthusiastic."

"Maybe that's the wrong word, but he's so gentle with the little kids, so—well—nice. He smiles a lot and I can see how well he connects with people. He's a good listener. Everywhere he goes, the older boys follow. He believes in the work of the shelter—really believes in it." Olivia took a slow drink. "He's wonderful."

"Whoa. I'm missing something here, girlfriend. He bawled you out for saying something to Mia and you get all starry-eyed and think he's wonderful?"

"That's just it. He didn't bawl me out. He came to see what happened, and then he said it would all work out." Olivia heard herself. "Don't get me wrong. He's not all that. I mean he calls me 'Chip' for the chip he says I carry on my shoulder."

"Oh, ouch."

"Yeah, it would sting if he didn't smile that gorgeous smile every time he said it." Olivia could picture that smile.

Jane set her drink down and looked straight at Olivia. "I asked you this once before, but are you crushing on him?"

"No. Not at all."

"You sure?"

"Once I resign, I'll hardly ever see him again."
Olivia sighed. "I need to try to catch Diane at youth
group tomorrow night."

"Speaking of youth group . . ." Jane fidgeted with
her napkin. "Aubrey asked Carter to come as well."

"Carter?"

"He said he'd be happy to come."

"Carter and Aubrey?"

Jane nodded her head.

Olivia looked down at her frappuccino. The foam
had gone completely flat.

Be Still

7

Gather round, everyone." Pastor Joe raised his voice so the kids playing foosball could hear. "Let's throw some of those pillows on the floor. Everyone get comfortable." The chill of cement under linoleum in the room where youth group met called for something soft and insulating. Plus, Pastor Joe encouraged them to be casual as they listened. Some kids would lounge on the pillows; others would scoot chairs over.

"If you don't have a mug of hot cider, come

over and get one before you settle in," Diane called to the group.

"I'll give you a couple minutes to get your drinks," Pastor Joe added.

Olivia helped Diane ladle the hot cider into mugs. They had a big group tonight, including both Aubrey and Carter. It seemed everywhere Carter went tonight, Aubrey chose the same activity. Olivia could practically see the initial *C* charm that would someday grace Aubrey's newest bracelet. *She'll probably choose the bling-bling of rhinestones for someone as hot as Carter.* Olivia shook her head. *What am I saying? You are losing it, girl —especially if you start talking to yourself all the time.*

"Hey, Chip. You look like you're miles away. Got a hot cider for a friend?" Carter stood in front of her.

How long has he been standing there? Good thing he doesn't read minds. "Sorry, I was lost in thought." She handed him a mug.

"You coming over to hear Pastor Joe's talk?"

"As soon as I get these handed out."

"I'll save you a place."

Aubrey stepped up next to him. "I've already got a big floor pillow for us, Carter. That guy in the corner's guarding it for me." She looked to the corner to smile and wiggle her fingers at one of the freshmen. "Unfortunately, there's not a lot of room there."

Carter seemed surprised but didn't say anything.

"That's OK." Olivia definitely did not want to sign on for another competition with Aubrey. *Stay far away from Aubrey—far, far away.* "I think Jane saved me a spot."

"Do you have anything that's not loaded with sugar, Olivia?" Aubrey slid her hand down her waist and hip. "It's a constant battle to keep fit."

I can't believe Aubrey's competition with me will now in-fect youth group as well. "I could get you a glass of water."

"Do you have bottled water?"

Diane came over. "I can tell you're a first-timer here, Aubrey. Welcome. It's either feast or famine here. The feasting times usually include large doses of chocolate, sugar, or other calorie-rich goodies. Unfortunately, we usually have famine, so eat up and enjoy while you can."

Pastor Joe gave another call for everyone to settle in. Aubrey passed on the cider, grabbed Carter by the hand, and pulled him toward the corner she'd already staked out.

Diane smiled and whispered to Olivia, "Carter doesn't look like he knows what hit him."

Olivia decided not to comment. She took a sponge, wiped up the stickiness on the goodie table, and headed over to the group. She squeezed in next to Jane—clear across the room from Carter and Aubrey.

How could Aubrey look so good and still look casual? She had a certain polish—just the right shade of lip gloss, the perfect touch of eye makeup. Her clothes always looked like everyone else's, only better. She might be wearing a pair of jeans with boots, but her jeans fit like a glove with that designer-kind-of-look. Olivia imagined that her boots must have come from Italy. *Stop it! You need to keep your mind far away from Aubrey.*

"Hurry up, everyone." Pastor Joe waited for the group to get their stuff and settle in. "Two-minute warning."

"I hope Aubrey likes youth group," Jane whispered. "She looks like she's having fun, doesn't she?"

Olivia looked at Aubrey again. She was staring up at Carter and doing that winding finger thing she did in her hair. "I'm trying very hard to keep out of Aubrey's line of sight."

"Why does Diane seem so funny?" Jane changed the subject.

"Funny?"

"She seems distracted or something. Did you tell her you're quitting?"

"No. I haven't had time." Olivia looked back at Diane. Jane was right. She did seem preoccupied—it wasn't like her. She usually sparkled. "I'm hoping to talk to her later."

"Time's up." Pastor Joe stood up as the group quieted. "Let's open with a word of prayer." He prayed, asking God to join them—to open hearts and stimulate minds. He also asked God to reassure those who suffered worry and anxiety.

What an unusual thing to pray for this group. Pastor Joe must know something about somebody in the group. Olivia added her prayers to his.

"This week, in my own devotions, I've been focusing on the words found in verse ten of Psalm forty-six. Let me read it. 'Be still, and know that I am God.'"

Olivia saw Carter settle in to listen. She could see that he really connected with Pastor Joe already.

"With school getting crazier, with midterms and papers staring you in the face, isn't it harder than ever to find your quiet time with God each day?"

He has no idea, thought Olivia. In September she'd listed daily quiet time as her number one priority. The first couple weeks of school, she'd done pretty well. Then it had been hit-and-miss, going downhill from there. Since Halloween, she'd been lucky to gather up books and homework to get out the door on time.

"Our lives get busier and busier," Pastor Joe continued. "But that's when we need that stillness the most. Other pseudoreligions and cults call it 'centering ourselves,' but we know the truth. It is *not* getting more into ourselves that we need."

Olivia took out her day planner, opening to her goals section.

"And the Lord doesn't instruct us to be still and to know Him because He somehow needs all eyes on Him. That's a human-type thing. He tells us to do this because He knows *we* need Him. He knows the quiet times with Him will get us in shape for the tough stuff."

Olivia underlined her first goal and squeezed the words "Recommitted to goal #1" and today's date next to it. Pastor Joe was right. She needed to meet with God every day. How could she expect to make it through without His strength? *I've failed miserably, Father. I need Your help to accomplish this.*

"Don't make the mistake of thinking tough times won't come to us. Many of you are believers already." He looked around the room. "Others are still searching. Let me make this clear: Even if you choose to follow Jesus, you're still going to have trouble in your life." He paused and seemed to look at Diane, who stood behind the group. "We need to make sure we're all prayed up and ready to take on the challenges."

He talked more about challenges and about the practical ways to accomplish a regular quiet time. "We grow the most in the tough times, not when everything is smooth sailing. Invest in being still, so you'll be ready to take on the tough assignments."

He had one of the guys close in prayer before he

shut his Bible and invited everyone to hang out, play
foosball, or talk for as long as they wished.

Olivia knew she needed to go talk to Diane about
her job at the shelter, but something didn't feel right.
She couldn't put her finger on it.

"That was a great message, wasn't it?" Carter came
over to where Olivia and Jane were getting up.

"It definitely challenged me," Olivia answered.
"Jane, have you met Carter?"

Jane put out her hand to Carter. "I've seen you
around, but I haven't really met you. I'm Jane."

"Hi, Jane. Nice to meet you." He smiled and the corners of his mouth crinkled. Olivia hadn't noticed how
soft his eyes looked when he smiled. His bottom lids
sort of came up—it was like his eyes smiled as well.

Aubrey's eyes narrowed. "Jane is my good friend—
the one I've been telling you about."

Jane looked uncomfortable.

"I liked Joe's message, too." Aubrey's finger went up
to a wisp of hair tucked behind her ear. Her bracelets
clinked together. "I'm going to do that centering myself
thing Joe mentioned."

Carter seemed ready to say something, but one of
the guys called to him to join the foosball group. He
said that he'd be right there. "I like your youth group
and I really like Joe Javier. We've been looking for a
church since we moved here to Bay Vista. I'm going to
get my dad to visit and see if he feels the same."

As he moved off, Diane called Olivia over. "Would
you mind doing the clean-up . . . maybe get a couple of
other girls to help?" Diane ran a hand through her hair.

"Are you OK, Diane?"

"I'm a little under the weather. I just need to go home. Joe and I brought separate cars."

"I'll be glad to clean up." Olivia looked hard at Diane. Jane was right. Something bothered Diane.

"Thanks. We'll talk at work and catch up then." Tears seemed to gather in her eyes. "I don't know what I'd do if I didn't have your help. You've been God's gift to me." Diane hugged her before gathering her things together and slipping out the door.

So much for plans to resign tonight. Olivia was glad she hadn't come right in and blurted it out. For some reason, this was not the time. A few more days wouldn't hurt.

Jane came over to help her with the clean-up. "Aubrey jumped in to say I was her friend before I could mention to Carter that we've been friends since kindergarten." She gave the table a swipe of the cloth. "I like Aubrey. She can be fun, but you will always be my best friend."

Olivia smiled. Jane was the best.

"We're still on for Tuesday, right? *Changing Faces?*"

"It's a date."

Later, as Olivia got out of Jane's car, she thought about what Pastor Joe said. Her schedule became more of a challenge with each passing week. She needed to keep the commitment to be still. It would be the only way she'd ever meet the crazy schedule ahead of her.

I need to remember to write Jane into my planner for Tuesday, she thought as she let herself into the house.

RealTV

Trouble Crowds In

8

"It's cold, isn't it?" Olivia caught up with Mia walking to the BART station.

Mia slowed her pace and the girls fell in together. "I'm just glad BART heats the trains," Mia said. "I don't remember this kind of cold so early. At least not in Los Angeles."

Olivia laughed. "I guess people back east would think we're crazy for complaining about the low fifties, but, after all, this is California."

The early chill reminded her that November had given way to December, and she still hadn't told Diane about her resignation. Lately, she worked alone or with Mia more often than not.

"I wonder what's up with Diane?" Olivia asked.

"My mother is worried. She says Mrs. Javier . . . Diane . . . seems distant these days."

"Your mom is worried?" Olivia thought back to the last few weeks. Diane had been hit-and-miss with youth group. When she was there, she seemed quiet and distant. When Olivia came to work, she'd usually find a note propped up on her table with things that needed doing along with a quick happy face or a "you are a godsend" comment. "What does your mother say?"

"She says to pray." Mia smiled. "But my mother is a worrier, so don't take what she says too seriously."

Olivia longed to ask Mia more questions about her mother and her family but held her tongue. She couldn't trust herself. She always came out with the wrong thing. That's why it was so important for her to find some other volunteer position besides the shelter. *Maybe I could tutor kids in reading or help grade papers for one of the teachers at school.*

"I keep hoping that as my mother learns to pray, she'll stop worrying so much. Like Pastor Joe says, we need to be 'anxious about nothing.'"

"What does your mom worry about besides Diane?" Olivia asked before she could stop herself.

"It would be easier to say what she doesn't worry about. She wants to get back to work—she's a preschool day care supervisor, you know."

"No, I didn't know." Olivia knew almost nothing about Mia. "Our church has a preschool. Why doesn't she apply there? I know Joe and Diane would recommend her."

Mia sighed deeply. "I figured Carter or Mrs. Jav . . . Diane . . . probably told you about us."

"No. They never talk about the shelter residents. I think it's because of privacy." Olivia felt uncomfortable. She glanced over at Mia without being obvious. The girl was tall and slender with wavy dark brown hair swinging with each step and her oversized black eyes averted as usual. Olivia wished they could be friends. She sensed a kindred spirit in Mia even though their backgrounds were so different.

The only way to make friends, though, was to open up to each other. It was almost like, until you shared some deep-down stuff, friendship stayed on a superficial level.

"My mother had to leave her job when she left my stepfather." Mia must have felt the same. She seemed to have decided to talk openly. "That's why I go to school in a totally different district from the shelter."

"I don't understand what one thing has to do with the other." Olivia couldn't seem to connect the dots in this picture, but she recognized that Mia was reaching out by sharing.

"My real father died when my brother was little. It was just the three of us for a couple of years. We lived in South Central L.A., and my mom worked in a Head Start there so she could be with my little brother." Mia shared this freely. It must have been an easier time. "That's when she met Carlos, my stepfather."

"Your stepfather?"

"Well, he wasn't my stepfather then. He came into our lives, and everything seemed better. He had lots of money, though that's not why my mother fell in love with him. He seemed so kind—like he would take care of us all." Mia seemed to be reliving it. "He even took us to Disneyland."

"What fun."

"It was. My mother said she felt like a girl again. She said yes when he asked her to marry him. His work took him away for long periods of time, so we never had time to see all the parts of him."

"His work?" Olivia didn't mean to ask more than she should, but she'd gotten caught up in the telling.

"He said he was a labor contractor—the man who would go into Mexico and hire crews of seasonal workers for agriculture. You know, farm workers," Mia explained. "It's a good job. It pays well because the farmers need someone to supply workers, someone who can work with the union. The workers need some-one who'll manage the work, keep the legal and immi-gration things in order, provide transportation, and line up the jobs."

"It sounds kind of like the management-type stuff my dad does as a building contractor."

"Except as time went on, things didn't add up. He did have some crews working, but not like other con-tractors. My mother began to suspect something. He had so much money—even off-season."

"What did she suspect?" The whole conversation made Olivia uneasy. This sounded like an action movie. She had no idea what would come next—drug smug-gling? International espionage? *Stop it. This is not the stuff of a movie. This is Mia's life. Her tragedy.*

"Have you ever heard of Coyotes?"

"Of course. I've even seen coyotes come out of the foothills looking for food."

"Not that kind of coyote." Mia smiled. For some

82

reason Olivia's answer seemed to break the tension. "I mean the men who take huge amounts of money to smuggle illegal aliens across the border."

"Oh, I just read about one in the newspaper who packed dozens of people in the back of a truck, and when he began to sense pressure from the authorities, he left the people locked in the truck with no air and no food in the desert. Didn't several die?"

"Yes." Mia closed her eyes for a second.

Stupid, stupid, stupid. Why do you always have to stick your foot in your mouth? "Oh, I didn't mean that like it was your stepfather or anything. . . ."

"It's OK, Olivia. That's exactly what my mother thought when she began to put two and two together. She's a very out-there person, so when he came home the next time, she came right out and asked him."

"That was brave."

"Or dumb. He became infuriated. It was the whole macho thing—the wife does not question the husband." Mia flinched. "He started hitting her. When my brother and I defended her, we got beaten as well."

"How awful, Mia."

"My mother left right then, and we ended up all the way up here—for safety. We know Carlos is searching for us—again, it's a macho thing."

"A macho thing?"

"I know it sounds like a stereotype, but it's a cultural thing. Most Hispanic men are good—family men who take a protective attitude toward their families."

"My dad does as well."

Mia nodded. "I know. I see that caretaker role in many Christian families I've watched since moving here."

"But how was it different for your stepfather?"

"He believes he somehow owns us and that my mother has no right to even question him—even if she suspects him of illegal dealings. When she left, he acted like he'd lost his property."

"How awful."

"He will never stop looking for us. He used to say that he would never forgive disloyalty in his ranks. 'Traitors never go unpunished,' he always said, or they would infect the whole operation."

Olivia didn't know how to reply. She felt frightened. No wonder Mia so often looked behind them as they walked or seemed to scan the BART train as they boarded.

"That's why my mother cannot seek work. He'll have people checking every preschool, every Head Start in the state."

"Oh, Mia—"

A car pulled up alongside them, and Olivia felt her stomach suddenly clench with fear.

"You ladies need a ride?"

Olivia turned at the familiar voice. It was Carter.

"I can save you the BART fare if you're willing to trust your lives to my driving." Carter tilted his head. "You two look like you think I'm the boogeyman."

Mia laughed. "We were deep in an intense conversation."

Carter got out of the car and came around to the passenger door. "Well, I wouldn't want to intrude on serious girl talk."

"Oh, stop." Olivia laughed. If he only knew what the conversation had been about. Olivia appreciated the interruption. She had no idea what she could say to Mia —*the fear that must hang over them* . . .

"Thank you, Carter. You take Olivia. I can't go with-out my mother's permission." Mia waved Olivia off.

"I'll take BART with Mia then." Olivia couldn't be-lieve she was turning down a warm ride.

"Why not just call the center and ask your mother, Maria Elena?" Carter handed her the phone. "It'll cut a half hour off your travel."

Mia took the phone and dialed. While she talked, Carter leaned against the car and looked at Olivia.

"What?" Olivia fought the urge to straighten her sweater and run a hand through her hair.

"You are something else."

"What, Carter?" She felt like squirming under his gaze until he smiled.

"My mother said it's fine." Mia handed the phone back to Carter, interrupting the confusing nonconversa-tion. "She thinks you practically walk on water."

Olivia didn't mean to snort, but her laugh came out in a little explosion.

"What's the matter, Chip? You don't agree?" Carter put his hands on his hips.

Mia climbed into the backseat and dumped her backpack on the seat beside her. "Why do you call her 'Chip'?"

"You heard that snort, Maria Elena, didn't you? This kid wears a chip on her shoulder. That snort was proof enough, was it not?" He took Olivia's backpack and pitched it in the back with Maria Elena's. When Olivia slipped into the front seat, he handed her the seat belt buckle and closed the door. He came around and got into the driver's seat and buckled his seat belt. "You all belted in, Maria Elena?"

"Yep."

"As I was saying, 'Chip' is a sort of anatomical malady."

Olivia rolled her eyes and shook her head. She'd never admit it, but Carter's teasing always put everyone at ease.

"Uh-oh, Carter," Mia said. "I may have to tell my mother you do *not* walk on water after all. To be torturing Olivia like that—"

"Oh, she earned it." Carter grinned at Olivia.

Olivia hit him with her day planner—glad he hadn't yet pulled away from the curb.

When they arrived at the shelter, Mia went to check in with her mother, and Carter headed off toward the gym with a trail of boys following him. Today Olivia remembered to notice the children playing in the entry. She must have worn a smile on her face because several of the children smiled at her. One of the girls held up a frizzy-haired Barbie for her fashion approval.

"Nice clothes. I like the way you used a paper towel for her sweater."

The girl beamed at the compliment.

Too bad I'm resigning today. Could I be getting the hang of this? Maybe all it takes is being aware of the people around me. She had to admit that Carter set a good example.

Diane wasn't in her office. *When will I ever get the chance to talk to her?* All the file folders on the upcoming benefit were out of the file cabinets and stacked on Olivia's table. An envelope with her name was propped on top of the stack.

How strange. Olivia opened the envelope, took out the letter, and read:

Dear Olivia,

How often I've thanked God that He sent you to the shelter at exactly this time. You may have sensed something is up since I've been gone so much lately. Besides, when I've been there, I know I must have seemed distracted. Thank you for holding down the fort for me.

I didn't want to say anything to anybody until I knew for sure—until now. I have been scheduled for surgery and will be out of the office for a while. Doctors discovered I have breast cancer, so it is to be immediate surgery and then probably a course of chemotherapy and radiation.

We need to talk about the benefit. I've spoken to Mrs. Bailey, and it looks like I'm going to try to direct the PR from the hospital and home as long as you are willing to be my contact person at the shelter.

I know it's a lot to ask, so think about it, talk to your mom and dad, pray about it, and then we'll talk. If you can come up to the hospital tonight, perhaps we can get a little strategy session in before my surgery.

You are a godsend to me, Olivia. Word of my surgery goes out on the prayer chain today, and Mrs. Bailey will let the residents and staff know as well.

See you soon?

Love,
Diane

Olivia stood the whole time she read the letter. She folded the letter and sank into her chair. No wonder Pastor Joe seemed to be communicating across the room with Diane as he gave his messages at youth group. What a burden they carried. At least now everyone would know and could be praying with them.

She was about to pick up the phone and call Jane when the door opened and Mia came in.

"What?" Mia came right over to the desk. "What happened, Olivia?"

"Read this." Olivia handed the envelope to Mia.

Mia read the letter and looked up with tears in her eyes. "That's why she's been gone so much."

"I had no idea. I wonder how bad it is? Do you think it's—?" Olivia couldn't put her fear into words.

"I don't know. Maybe Pastor Joe and Diane don't know yet either. I do know that most cancers can be cured these days if they're caught soon enough. I saw a show on television about it. Even in the last five years they've made *mucho* progress."

"You're right. I'm just scared—Diane is such a friend—she's always been there for all of us. The C-word practically takes your breath away." Olivia took all the files and slid them into a canvas bag. "I'm going to take these home and go over them with my parents and see if they'll take me up to the hospital tonight."

"I'm going to talk to my mother. I know she'll want me to continue to help you with the PR stuff. She'll get the women here to start praying for Diane."

Olivia grabbed her backpack and the bag of files and headed back toward the reception room. Just as she was about to leave, she saw Carter sitting on the stairs leading up to the residence rooms. His legs were spread apart with his arms crossed on his knees and his head down on his arms.

"Carter. Are you OK?" She knew he was not OK. Something was wrong.

He took a deep breath in through his nose. "No." He paused. "I mean, yes."

Olivia was worried. Carter always seemed in charge.

"I heard about Diane, and it hit me hard. So much for faith . . . I completely panicked. Give me a minute."

"I know. It's so scary. I'm going to get my parents to take me up to the hospital. Diane asked me to cover for her here at the shelter. I have no idea how I'm going to manage. I need my mom to help me figure it out." Olivia knew she talked in circles—covering up her discomfort with Carter's reaction.

"Come on. I'll give you a ride home." He smiled. "I'm OK now. Having a friend diagnosed with breast cancer just takes me back . . . my mom, you know." Carter took the backpack from her. "Someday I'll tell you about it."

She didn't even want to think about Diane and Carter's mother at the same time. Olivia only wanted to hear happy survivor stories.

9

Have Yourself a Harried Little Christmas

"Olivia, you are late for dinner again." Mom laid her fork beside her plate. "I know it's hard to get home on time from the shelter the days your father cannot pick you up, but you *have* to try."

"Your mother's right. Dinner together is a top priority." Her dad smiled. "Come on, put your things down, and let's eat."

"I'm sorry, Mom, Dad. I'm trying as hard as I can, but it does not seem to be enough." Olivia felt close to tears.

Tank looked at her, but he didn't say a

word. Olivia knew she must seem an emotional wreck for Tank to restrain himself from making comments.

"When we told you we'd help you stay on at the shelter—for Diane's sake—maybe we allowed you to take on too much." Mom looked worried.

"I don't know." Olivia took a bite of salad. "If it weren't for the shelter, I'd probably have taken on something else. I seem to be congenitally unable to balance my life."

"Are you still making time for your quiet time, honey?" Dad asked.

"You would have to ask that." Olivia rubbed her forehead. "Pastor Joe gave us a great talk about regular time for prayer and Bible study, and I pledged to make it a priority."

Tank rolled his eyes. He hated hearing about Olivia's priorities, schedules, or systems.

"Good. So you are putting God first. All the other things—"

"I intended to put God first, Dad. I even wrote a recommitment note on my goals sheet, but I've been having to finish up homework or study for tests in the morning, and I keep slipping farther and farther behind."

"Let me get you up a little earlier tomorrow, Olivia, and let's pray together for new resolve." Mom passed her the rice pilaf.

"Thanks, Mom. Maybe it will help jump-start me. I need all the help I can get."

They went on to other topics, including Tank's grades—a subject that always provided comic relief of sorts. Even though Olivia and her brother complained about eating dinner together, by the end of each meal they were always glad they did. Mom tried to make it fun.

"Sherman, if you give one more bite to that dog under the table, I will make you sit under the table and eat with him," Mom said.

"We are decorating for Christmas this Saturday. You'll be off early, right? Plan to spend the evening here in our own tinsel town," Dad announced.

"Should work out fine. I'm scheduled at the shelter from nine to noon. Mia and I are planning how many different appeals we'll generate before the benefit. We need to get it all calendared before the new year."

"Now that's a new verb—calendared," Mom said. "It sounds like good planning. When you told us about Diane's medical crisis, don't forget that I told you I'd help."

"I remember, but I know how busy you are. I'm trying to get it all under control." She got up to help clear the table. "I'm going to hit the books right after dishes. You have no idea . . ."

☆   ☆   ☆

"Jane?" Olivia decided to take a minute to touch base with Jane after looking at her goals page and seeing that note about Jane. Guilt made her put off homework in order to call. "What are you doing?"

"It's not the elusive Olivia, is it?"

Olivia decided to ignore the jab. "I didn't see you at lunch today. Were you making up a test or something?"

"No."

"Where were you?"

"Are you volunteering for the attendance office or

something?" Jane gave a laugh but it was away from the phone. She sounded so distant.

"Looks like I caught you at a bad time. I'll let you go. I just wondered if you were coming over for *Changing Faces* tomorrow."

"Tomorrow?" Jane paused. Olivia heard the muffled sound of voices. Jane must have her hand over the receiver. "Uh, Aubrey invited me to come watch it on her new plasma TV. I figured you'd be busy." She sounded embarrassed.

"Oh."

"Why don't you come watch it with us? I'm sure Aubrey won't mind."

"I'd better not—rides and all. Have fun. Maybe I'll see you tomorrow. If you're eating lunch, that is. I've gotta go." She sounded more like Jane with that nervous rush of words. All she wanted was to get off the phone.

"Bye . . ." Jane sounded funny.

Olivia clicked the phone off. *That was too weird.*

She sat on the middle of her bed and wrapped her comforter around her. *I don't even want to think about this.* She popped a leftover chocolate candy in her mouth. *I will read Hamlet; and I will outline my paper; and I will go to bed—in that order.*

☆   ☆   ☆

"You have no idea how much I appreciate the ride home." It was Saturday, and Olivia expected to leave the shelter at noon, take BART home, and have all afternoon for homework. Now, here it was—after six and pitch-black outside.

"I hope you're not in a hurry to get home?" Carter seemed to be hitting every red light between Hayward and Bay Vista.

"You have no idea," Olivia said. "Dinnertime at my house is sacrosanct, and it is always held precisely at six on the dot."

"Oops."

"And tonight we are decorating for Christmas immediately afterward. My dad made a point of reminding me to be on time." She sighed and shook her head. "What am I doing wrong?"

"I'm not sure you're doing anything wrong. I see you doing a lot of things right." Another red light. Carter looked over at her and shrugged his shoulders. "It would be like me thinking these red lights are my fault. Things just happen."

"I know. It's just that red lights don't bother you if you leave enough time."

"Good point." Carter reached over and touched her hand. "Don't forget, Chip, that you are going to school and trying to do an almost-full-time job."

Olivia felt a tightness in her throat. "Oh, Carter, whatever you do, don't be nice to me. I'm so tired, I'm liable to dissolve into tears."

"OK. I'll go back to being mean. I just wanted to say that as I watch you work, I'm amazed at what you accomplish." He looked over at her and smiled. "Consider me harsh and critical once more."

Olivia laughed. *As if . . .*

"Here we are. Do you want me to go inside with you to 'splain things to your folks?"

"Thanks for the offer, but I'll walk this plank alone. If we both climbed out there, we'd just make a bigger splash before drowning." She opened the door and stepped out.

Carter laughed as he leaned over to shut the door. "See you tomorrow at youth group? Or should I come and fish you out of the drink first?"

She laughed and gave a quick noncommittal wave as she slipped inside.

Her dad was on the phone. "Olivia," he said as he covered the phone. "We've been worried sick." He spoke into the phone, "Thank you, Mrs. Bailey. She just walked in the door." He paused to listen. "Sorry to bother you at home."

Yikes. Dad called the shelter director at home. Why didn't I take time to find a pay phone to call instead of bemoaning the fact that I don't have a cell phone? "Sorry, Dad, Mom. I'd planned to get off at noon—"

"We don't want another apology or another excuse." Mom rarely interrupted. *She must be furious.*

"May I put my things in my bedroom and then tell you what happened?"

"Why don't we tell *you* what happened? We expected you home in the early afternoon. Dad planned a special treat for all of us—cutting down the Christmas tree at a tree farm in the foothills. We made reservations for afternoon tea at Tyme for Tea in Niles afterward." Mom spoke slowly and deliberately.

"When you didn't come, we called the shelter, and the receptionist said you'd left at about one." Dad paced as he spoke. "We waited and waited, and then we started calling around. Jane said she hasn't seen you for days. We didn't want to bother Pastor Joe, but if you hadn't come, he would have been next."

Mom continued. "We were so excited about planning

a special surprise. The excitement turned to worry about three o'clock and by five, panic had set in."

Tank piped in, "I sat here all day waiting for you. If you weren't coming, I could have gone with Jason to the mall, but no-o . . ."

"That's enough, Sherman." Dad might be completely comfortable chewing Olivia out, but he drew the line at letting Tank grouse. "So, where were you?"

"What does it matter now?" Olivia had been on the verge of tears for days. They could be denied no longer. "I'm sorry. I'm sorry. I ruined everything."

"I expect an explanation," Dad said.

"You said you didn't want excuses. My explanation will just sound like another pack of excuses." Her tears were running off her chin, and she felt as if she were moving on to the big gulpy sobs. "What does it matter?" She headed for her room.

"Young lady—" Dad started.

"Give her a minute, Jack," she heard her mother say.

In her room, Olivia dropped her things on the floor by the door and threw herself across the bed. She hated dramatics and had never been one to run to her room in tears, but this time she desperately needed sanctuary.

Lord, what can I do? If I do a good job in one area, I'm going to mess up in another. Please help me. Please.

She lay there in the darkened room until she could breathe away the sobs. Her chest hurt, but smashing her face into the bedspread felt so good, she couldn't bring herself to move.

Now, how to end this rift with my family? That was the worst thing about coming undone. Do you slink back and apologize? Do you wait for someone to come into your room to check on you? She knew her parents were probably miserable as well.

When she was little, she'd write a note and slip it under her door into the hallway. Her parents would get the note and come in to finish the talk. *I guess slipping a note under the door is not exactly seventeen-year-old behavior.*

She got up, wiped off her face, and rejoined her family. Her mother patted the couch next to her. Puggles came up and pushed against her with his cold nose.

"I am so sorry for ruining this day. I'm also sorry for not calling."

"Apology accepted. As busy as you are, we probably should have spelled out the plans and not tried to surprise you." Dad tugged on a piece of her hair. "We got so worried that something had happened—that maybe you were in an accident or something. When you came in without a scratch, we practically wanted to kill you."

Mom laughed. "It doesn't make sense, but you'll understand when you are a parent."

Tank and Puggles rolled on the carpet together, making everything seem normal once again.

"Let's go back to where we started," Dad said. "What happened to detain you?"

"Mia and I worked on the letters and ads that will need to be done in the first quarter of the year. We came across several of the ad contracts and noticed that they had to be signed and the ads booked by Monday to reserve ad space. We had no choice other than to take them up to the hospital to have Diane sign them."

"You should have called," Mom said. "I could have given you a ride."

"I know. I should have called. Carter had finished

open gym, though, and offered. It seemed like the quickest way." Olivia sighed. "Even though you expected me home in the early afternoon, I thought the deadline was still dinner at six."

Dad raised his eyebrows.

"I know, I know. I was late for the six o'clock deadline as well, but close—sort of within reason." Olivia gave the crooked grin that she'd always used when trying to wheedle something out of her parents.

"Anyway, I'm so sorry for ruining the surprise. In fact, I feel miserable that I missed out on the day—it sounds exactly like my kind of day. I can almost taste the scones." Olivia wished she had known.

"It's not all bad," Mom said. "The good news is that we were able to get the same reservation for tomorrow, so be ready to leave directly after church, and we'll have you back in time for youth group."

"Dad and I will set the tree up while you are at youth group, and when you get home, we'll decorate." Tank had Puggles on his lap and made the dog's mouth move as if Puggles were speaking.

Yep. Everything is as normal as this family ever gets. Olivia felt so relieved.

"Thank you, Mom. Thank you, Dad."

"What about me?" Tank asked.

"Thank you, Puggles."

Mom patted Olivia's hand. "Honey, you are carrying a huge load. When I visited Diane, she told me what a superb job you are doing. Please let Dad and me help if we can."

"That's right," Dad said. "We still insist on keeping dinner and doing things together, but we are also a family that helps each other, aren't we?"

"Thanks." Olivia didn't want to end up blubbering again. "I'll definitely ask." She looked over toward the dining room. "Speaking of asking . . . is there any way for a latecomer to rustle up some dinner?"

Dreams Come True

10

"Can I give you a ride to the shelter to-day?" Jane had been waiting at Olivia's locker. "I happen to have a full tank of gas and nowhere to go."

Olivia looked at her friend. It had been way too long. "You've got a deal!" She felt like hugging Jane. "I'll even give you a couple of dollars to replace some of that precious gas."

"Or, if you could spare a half hour or so, we could use those dollars to get a hot chocolate at Frida's."

"If I get a ride, I'm already shaving about

thirty minutes off my commute. Don't get me started on my need for wheels. Yes, I'd love to stop for something hot. I'm so ready for spring to come."

"I need to go to my locker and get my stuff. I'll meet you in the parking lot."

Olivia ran to find Mia. "Jane asked me to stop for something to drink on the way to the shelter, so don't wait for me."

Mia and Olivia had grown their friendship over the weeks working together, so Mia knew how much Olivia missed her longtime friend. "*Muy bueno.* I'm so glad. Have fun."

"Want me to bring you a hot chocolate?"

"Mmmmm, yes. Can you sprinkle a little cinnamon on the top and leave off the whipped cream?"

Olivia headed out toward the parking lot and saw Jane loading her things in her car. "OK, I'm here."

"Chuck your stuff and climb in," Jane said as she settled herself into the driver's seat. "I decided if I was going to see you, I'd have to practically arrange a kidnapping. I can't believe we went through the whole Christmas vacation with only one afternoon together."

"I know. I miss you, Jane."

As they pulled out of the parking lot, Olivia saw Aubrey out of the corner of her eye. *Uh-oh.* Aubrey looked stunned. She stopped and put her hands on her hips. Her body language boded trouble. *Don't even go there. Remember? You are ignoring Aubrey.*

"Did I miss something?" Jane asked.

Olivia turned around. "Just Aubrey going out to her car. Are you still spending a lot of time together?" *Sheesh! That ignore-Aubrey resolve lasted less than a second.*

"Off and on. I'm glad she's coming to youth group,

and she can be a lot of fun, but she's definitely not Olivia." Jane did that little bam-bam-bam thing on Olivia's arm. "Aubrey spends so much time talking about you, I decided I'd rather talk to you for once instead of talk about you."

Oh, it felt good to be with crazy, fun Jane. "Are you wearing that lip gloss we got at Sephora? It looks so good."

"How come you're not wearing any of the stuff we bought? I've been looking at you and thinking I need to take you in hand again."

Olivia laughed. "You think I'm looking bad, eh?"

They pulled into the shopping center parking lot and made their way toward Frida's. "I can always tell how gruesome your schedule is by your grooming habits." She went into her upper-crust English accent for the grooming habits pronouncement.

"And, pray tell, what is wrong with my 'grooming habits'?"

"Come, get your chocolate, and Dr. Jane will prescribe."

They sat down, and Jane continued, "This scraping your hair back with a scrunchie is getting old. Didn't I teach you better than that?"

Olivia laughed. "And?"

"And the rumpled state of your clothes makes me think you are back to recycling from the floor of your closet."

"You are too cruel. Unfortunately, you are also too close. I'm so out of time for doing laundry, I'll confess to settling for rumples once or twice."

"What would Kinni say?"

"I know *Changing Faces* is in rerun for a while, but let's get together next week for it, anyway. OK?"

"It's a date!"

"Before we go, I need to get a hot chocolate for Mia."

"Mia?"

"Maria Elena, from the shelter. She's been helping me. She's an amazing translator."

"I think I have her in one of my classes. She's quiet."

"Until you get to know her. You'd love her."

"Speaking of loving your friends, what's up with Carter?"

Olivia inhaled deeply. "I wish I had time to find out. We are both so busy. But he is wonderful. I hope we'll be friends forever."

"Wow. You're not just crushing here, are you?"

"Not really. Friendship is much deeper than that. That's why today means so much to me. Thank you for kidnapping me." Olivia paused. "How I've missed you."

"Me too." They got in the car and buckled up. Jane started the engine. "You didn't thank me for torturing you about your grooming habits!"

☆   ☆   ☆

Mia beat Olivia into the office. She was happy to get the hot chocolate, putting both hands around the cup. "I don't know what's better, the taste or the warmth. Thank you. How much do I owe you?"

"*Nada*. Thanks for holding down the fort until I got here."

Mia smiled. "*Nada?* You scare me, Olivia. Was that

Español coming out of your mouth? Am I rubbing off on you?"

"Today must be my day to be tormented by friends." Olivia picked up a file off the desk. "Diane found this small print shop owner who has his finger on the pulse of the whole Hispanic community here. Do you think your mother will let you go meet him and try to sweet-talk him into printing our Spanish appeals *por nada?*"

Mia looked at the address. "Sure, it's close. Let me check with my mom. She may want to go with me. She still worries in case my stepfather . . . you know."

"I wish that didn't always hang over you. If you're sure you want to go, your goal is not just to get the printing. See if you can encourage the printer to become a friend of the shelter. We need him to come to the benefit and bring key people from the Hispanic community."

Mia smiled. "You're beginning to sound like a genuine publicity person now." She drank the last of her chocolate, picked up the file and a stack of brochures about the center, and left.

"Hey, Chip." Carter put his head in the door. "Mrs. Bailey wants to see you."

"Me?" Olivia couldn't imagine why the shelter director needed to see her. Mrs. Bailey dealt mostly with the benefactors, the board of directors, social workers, and the regulatory committees. "Do you think there's more trouble with Diane?"

"I don't think so." Carter still looked tense anytime they discussed Diane's battle with cancer. "No. We saw Pastor Joe last night, and didn't you visit her last week?"

"You're right." Olivia knew she had to stop worrying. Diane kept telling them that things looked good and she was healing well. She said they were doing the chemotherapy and radiation as a precaution—a double whammy to make sure she remained cancer-free.

"I know how you can find out what Mrs. Bailey wants." Carter had that sparkle in his eye. "Why not walk down to her office, knock on the door, and see if you can pry it out of her?"

Olivia picked up the little Nerf ball that sat beside her phone and aimed it straight toward the door.

"Missed me by a mile," Carter said as he headed off toward the gym. "Maybe I need to schedule some hoop time for you. Think you can pencil it in?"

Why did he always make Olivia smile? As she confided to Jane, she didn't have time to explore her feelings for him, but she knew she looked forward to seeing him at the shelter each time she worked.

✿   ✿   ✿

"Olivia. Good. Come in, come in." Mrs. Bailey stood up, smoothed down the straight skirt of her dark wool suit, and gestured to one of the chairs. "Please, have a seat."

Olivia had never been in this office. It was not as spartan as Diane's office but also nothing like Dad's plush office at the construction company headquarters. Olivia sat down.

"I hear such good things about your work. Diane reports that the work is moving along in an organized, intentional flow." Mrs. Bailey's voice reflected the executive manner she always maintained. "That says a lot for you. We keep reminding ourselves that you are still a high school student."

Olivia looked down at her hands. She knew she must be blushing, and she felt a little close to tears again. "Thank you, Mrs. Bailey."

"The directors asked numerous questions about the way you managed to incorporate one of our residents into the operation of the shelter. They feel it may be an important model for the future." She made conscious eye contact with Olivia. "They continue to take note."

"You're talking about Mia—Maria Elena—right?" Olivia knew she needed to correct this assumption. "That had nothing to do with me. Diane first called on Mia to help. And there was no thought given to trying to give Mia a job for her own sake. She's a better translator than we could ever afford, and she has a way of carrying herself and representing the shelter—"

"We know all that, but thank you for clarifying it. We know Maria Elena is above average in skills and intellect, but you'd be surprised at how many of our residents are equally gifted. Maria Elena's involvement reminded us of that." Mrs. Bailey smiled. "Whether you did this purposefully or not, the board is impressed with your work. They know that you must have recently applied for college admission. Mr. Wylie asked for a list of your college choices so the board can write them a letter on your behalf. He's also prepared a letter for the graduation committee at your school."

Olivia was speechless. She felt those familiar tears pricking her eyelids. Good thing she never had time for makeup. "I–I–thank you." She stood up to leave. "I'll get my list for Mr. Wylie. Thank you."

"No. Please sit down." Mrs. Bailey came out from behind the desk and propped herself against the front corner. "That was not even what I brought you in to talk about. I've been meaning to call you in to talk about the board's comments for a while but haven't had time."

Olivia smiled. Boy, did she understand that.

"I brought you in to tell you of a very interesting development that could mean unprecedented publicity for The Shelter of His Wing."

Olivia opened her planner to take notes.

"Diane first made inquiries last summer, shortly after last year's benefit. She wrote the producers with a proposal but never heard back. Before she could follow it up—"

"Excuse me, Mrs. Bailey, I'm lost. Producers?"

"Let me start all over. I need to collect my thoughts. This is so exciting, I'm getting ahead of myself."

Olivia had never seen Mrs. Bailey flustered. She was always in control—even in a crisis. What was this?

"Let me cut to the chase, and we'll do the details afterward." She stood up and resettled herself against the desk. "A television program called *Changing Faces* contacted us and offered to do a makeover for our public relations director to air just prior to the benefit. Much of the color commentary—"

"The B-roll."

"Yes, that's the word. Much of the B-roll will be shot here at the shelter. At the end of the show, they will include our info in the credits if people want to donate."

"*Changing Faces?*"

"Yes. Have you ever seen the show?"

"My friend, Jane, and I have never missed an episode."

"Now that you mention it, I think I remember Diane saying that. In fact, I think it was you who made

108

Diane think of proposing this." Mrs. Bailey shook her head as if to clear the cobwebs so she could get back on track. "Anyway, they want you to fly down in February. If we agree, they will be up here to shoot the—what do they call it again? Umm, the B-roll, week after next. Can your mother accompany—?"

"Me?" Olivia couldn't get her mind around this. "They wanted the public relations director."

"Diane already called them and told them about her leave of absence. You know Diane. She actually told them she was slightly 'hair-challenged' at the moment."

Olivia laughed. Leave it to Diane. No wonder everyone loved her. Forget that the chemo was starting to do a job on her hair. She would find a way to joke about it.

"So Diane already got the approval to substitute her 'young assistant publicist.' In fact, I believe she already sent some photos. Something like before-shots."

Olivia could just imagine what kind of before-shots Diane had collected. "It's going to take me some time to absorb this." Olivia didn't want to sound like a total airhead. She wrote a couple of words in her planner just to try to ground herself. "February? I will have to speak to my mother and father and then make sure I can be excused from school."

School! She was already behind and had planned to pull several late-nighters to catch up. *How will I add yet another thing?* Olivia paused in her mental gymnastics. *Are you crazy? We're talking* Changing Faces *here.*

"Can you have your mother call me at home tonight? I need to let the producer know by tomorrow." She took her card and wrote her home number on it. "I'll wait for the call."

Olivia left the office feeling as if she might wake at

any moment. *You never wonder if you are dreaming when you are in the middle of a real dream, do you?* She knew she made very little sense. *Stop it. Get ahold of yourself, girl. This is real. Unbelievable but real.*

Changing Faces! She could imagine what Jane would say. *Yikes, Jane! Changing Faces* had always been a Jane-Olivia thing. How would she ever tell Jane?

I'm here." Jane opened the front door and stuck her head inside.

"I guess I don't have to say come in. Puggles, stop barking. You make my ears bleed. This is just Jane. You've known Jane since you could barely waddle out of your basket."

"Some welcome! I guess it proves I've not been over here enough lately."

"That's the truth." Olivia went to turn on the television. She knew this episode was a rerun, but she had to somehow tell Jane her news without hurting her. She'd worried all weekend long.

Mom had given her wholehearted approval for the *Changing Faces* segment and agreed to make the trip with Olivia. In fact, Mom was looking forward to it. She planned to begin rearranging her February schedule this week.

When Mom called Mrs. Bailey, they had talked for a long time. The directors at the center considered this a major opportunity. Mom planned to take care of the school permissions tomorrow. Olivia knew that as soon as Mom spoke to the office, word would get out. Olivia had asked her to wait until Jane could be told.

"So . . . turn on the TV, O." Jane sat on the floor, her back against the couch, and her legs under the coffee table.

"Sorry. My mind's been less than focused lately." Olivia took the remote and switched the TV on and then scrolled down to the *Changing Faces* channel. "Here goes." She plopped onto the couch, immediately remembering that Mom asked her not to plop. Plopping came so naturally.

"Brilliant. I love this one. Puggles, puppy, you are cuter than this girl in her before-shots. I believe you may even have less wrinkles."

Puggles snuggled up next to Jane on the floor.

"At the next commercial break, I have something to announce." There, she said it. Olivia figured Jane would try to pry it out of her immediately.

"Have you hooked up with Carter?" Jane laid her head back on the couch, trying to see Olivia without turning around. "Aubrey will put out a contract on you."

"That's *not* my news, but why would Aubrey care? I see Carter enough to know he cannot possibly have enough time to be seeing Aubrey."

"But that's not for want of her trying. Aubrey's fun and all, but she really has this thing with you. I wish you guys could somehow mend this." Jane looked back at the TV and started talking to the screen. "Oh, no, Kinni. What are you thinking about? You cannot possibly have consented to wear that!"

"It does make her look a little Britney-like, doesn't it?" Olivia didn't want to even get into the Aubrey thing. She had planned to totally ignore her this year— it was written right in her goals—but she kept allowing herself to be reeled back into the fray. Plus, she felt weird about the relationship between Aubrey and Jane. It seemed like Aubrey was friends with Jane to somehow spite Olivia. That might not be fair to either one of them, but what about that look on Aubrey's face in the parking lot when she and Jane drove out?

I have no right to be worrying about Jane and Aubrey. As if I spend enough time with Jane. And now I have to tell Jane about Changing Faces.

". . . And the world does *not* need a thirty-five-year-old Britney." Jane laughed. The before-photos began to play. "This girl is going to kill her friends. If I was on *Changing Faces* and you sent a bathing suit photo, they'd have to put you into the Witness Protection Program."

What sort of pictures did Diane have? What if she had those shots taken on the houseboat trip last summer? What kind of bathing suit did I wear? Could she have taken photos when we had that all-girl slumber party and gave each other facials? Why did the facial mask have to be green?

"You are a million miles away." Jane craned her neck to look at Olivia. "I hope your news has nothing scary in it. It's not about Diane, is it?"

"No. Diane's doing pretty well." Olivia absently reached over to French-braid Jane's hair like she used to. "Wasn't that terrifying? The thought that we might lose her . . ."

"Pastor Joe will never be the same. You can see the softness in his eyes when he looks at her or when he talks about her." Jane leaned her head back toward Olivia. "That feels so good. How long has it been since we had a hair fest?"

"Too long." Olivia loved to French-braid, especially fine hair like Jane's. She found the rhythm soothing as her baby fingers parted and sectioned while her thumb and forefinger plaited the strands.

"I just hope somebody looks at me that way someday." Jane's voice sounded wistful.

"Huh?" Olivia had been braiding and watching Kinni criticize every outfit in the guest's wardrobe. "Looks at you like what?"

"You're not following. We were talking about Pastor Joe and Diane. I pray that someday someone will look at me like Joe looks at Diane."

"Me too. I wonder if that kind of love only really grows out of the kind of tough times they've been living through?" Olivia thought about it. "I mean, I know they've always loved each other, but this is something different. I see it in Carter's eyes."

"Carter looks at you like that?" Jane turned so sharply she pulled the braid right out of Olivia's hand. "He looks at you like that and you've never told me?"

"No, that's not what I mean. Carter lost his mother to cancer when he was little. I see that softness and longing come into his eyes when he talks about his mother." Olivia began undoing the braid. "Diane's cancer hit him especially hard. We haven't really been able to talk about it, but he seems so vulnerable somehow. I think Diane understands."

"How sad." Jane rubbed Puggles's head. "Look. Kinni's winding up the 'before' segment. Time for the commercial and your big news."

"OK, are you ready for this?"

"No. Let me guess first."

"You'll never guess."

"You heard you are going to be valedictorian."

"No."

"Your parents decided they are sending Tank to military boarding school."

"Nice try."

"Oh, I know! Your parents finally decided to get you a car."

"If only . . ."

"OK, does it have to do with college acceptances?"

"Jane, you will never guess."

"All right, I give. Let me go to the kitchen and get something to drink, and then I'm all ears." She managed to crawl out from her spot on the floor and head into the kitchen. "You want something?"

"No."

Olivia heard the refrigerator door open and the sound of a bottle being set on the tile counter.

"Did you finish your research paper in English?" Jane grunted.

She must be popping the top off the bottle, thought Olivia. Yep, she heard the pop. "No. I cannot even stand to think about the schoolwork that is piling up." Things seem to be spinning out of control schedulewise. Whenever she thought about the work she had to do, her stomach clenched and her neck muscles tightened. *How in the world can I ever fit in my work at the shelter, my schoolwork, and now this trip?*

"Hey. What are these? Airplane tickets?" Jane stopped talking. "LAX? You and your mom are going to Los Angeles in February?" She walked into the room with a confused look on her face. "The envelope underneath those tickets was sent overnight to you last week—"

"You'd make a great detective. That was the news I was trying to tell you." Olivia could see from Jane's face that waiting to tell her was a mistake.

"But this is Tuesday. You are planning a trip to L.A. with your mother, and you wait several days to tell me?" Jane's voice carried a note of hurt in it.

"I wanted to tell you in person." It sounded like a lame excuse when she said it.

"In the old days, you would have called, and I would have driven right over." Jane sat down on the couch. "OK, shoot. I'm flat out of guesses."

"First, let me come clean." Olivia knew that she'd be stumbling all over her words if she didn't. "I delayed because I couldn't bear to tell you. I've been making myself sick over how to tell you."

"Since when do you have to worry about how to word things to me?" Jane shook her head. "I'm totally lost. What could be so hard to tell me?"

"Well, it's not hard to tell you. It's just that it should be you and not me."

Jane threw up her hands in exasperation. "Will you please just tell me?"

"I'm going to Hollywood to be a guest on *Changing Faces.*" There. She'd said it.

Jane sat stunned. "No way!" She stood up and walked across the room before turning to look at Olivia. "No way! No way!"

"Jane? Are you upset?"

"I'm furious that you thought I'd be upset, but this is brilliant! Fantastic!"

"And I worried about this all weekend?" Olivia felt relieved. She should have known that Jane would be happy for her.

"I am also upset that you thought I needed a makeover more than you. Puhlease." Jane tried to make it a joke, but Olivia could tell that she'd hurt Jane by not making her part of the excitement from the very beginning.

"I didn't mean you needed the makeover. It's just that we always watched *Changing Faces* together, and it seemed weird to be going alone."

"How did this happen, anyway?"

Olivia told her about Mrs. Bailey and Diane and the offer. Jane kept shaking her head.

"All I can say is, brilliant. It's lit-rally brilliant."

"I should have known you'd be behind me, Jane. Forgive me for doubting you."

"Forgiven."

The way she dismissed the apology and whipped out the reply made Olivia know the hurt went deep. What could she do to mend this?

"When do you leave? You need to call me and talk to me from L.A. I want to be with you every step of the way, even if it's only by phone." Jane barely stopped to catch her breath. "Don't let them do anything harsh."

Olivia tried to match Jane's tone. "I figured you'd consider anything an improvement." She'd figure out what to do to mend the hurt feelings later, when she had some time to think about it.

What I really need to do is pray about it. How many times did I promise God to spend time regularly with Him? I'm blowing it in nearly every area of my life.

They watched the rest of the show together. Jane gave Olivia more advice than she could ever absorb. How Olivia wished Jane was as OK as she sounded. Trouble is, they'd known each other too long to bluff.

✫   ✫   ✫

"I don't know what I would have done if you hadn't taken pity on me and given me a ride." Olivia tried to calm her nervousness. She smoothed her hands on her skirt, hoping the moisture wouldn't leave marks.

"I'm happy to do it. I have to be there, anyway." Carter still talked in that slow, calm way. "You're not nervous, are you?"

"Don't tell me you're not."

He smiled. "If I'm not nervous already, you're going to make sure I get there, right?"

"Mia stayed home this morning. She didn't see any sense in coming all the way to Bay Vista just for one period." Olivia figured if she talked about something besides the B-roll filming, she'd feel better. "I wish I had been able to bring Jane."

"I guess they wanted to script it so closely around the shelter, they felt they had enough faces without hers."

"But I love her face."

Carter laughed. "Your mom is coming over directly from her hospital thing?"

"Yes. Today is her hospital volunteer day, so she

thought she'd get a few hours in there. She's swinging by to pick up Diane on the way."

"I hope it's not too much for Diane."

"She's such a part of the story; I'm glad she'll be in the B-roll at least.

"I love the shelter, but I sort of wish the B-roll could have been shot somewhere else. The chaos of all the kids running through and—"

Carter looked at her without smiling. "When you get nervous, that chip sort of gets prominent, doesn't it?"

Olivia looked down at her skirt. It looked positively rumpled. She'd tried her best to look good today. She secretly hoped she'd look good enough so when the be-fore footage came on, people would wonder how they could possibly improve on her.

"A penny for your thoughts."

She wouldn't say how much that last comment hurt. She'd always said the work of the shelter was not within her comfort zone. Sometimes the stretching everyone kept talking about hurt. Better to joke than to get into it today. "You must have learned that penny stuff from your grandmother. With inflation, I need at least enough to get a latte."

"OK, a buck thirty-five for your thoughts."

"I was just thinking I look pretty forlorn and entirely before-ish."

Carter looked over at her. "I think you look just right. I can't imagine what they could do to improve you."

"You need to consider politics as a career choice. But thank you for saying exactly the right thing. You have no idea how much I needed a little compliment right now."

"I shouldn't have said that about a chip on your shoulder. You are doing a great job even if all the pandemonium of the shelter gets under your skin." He laughed again. "When I get nervous, I snipe."

When they arrived at the shelter, they couldn't believe the confusion. It made the usual chaos seem orderly by comparison. The *Changing Faces* truck was parked directly in front of the shelter, and people were moving from the truck to the entrance and back again. From a distance it looked like a stream of ants heading toward a picnic.

This is not going to be a picnic, however. Help me stay calm amid the commotion, Lord. Olivia looked around to see if she could spot Kinni McKay. *She must wait until the last minute.*

By asking around, Olivia found out that much of the raw footage had already been shot—stills of the center in which the crew promised to carefully disguise the location; quick interviews with Mr. Wylie, Mrs. Bailey, and Diane.

They wanted to get film of Carter working in the gym with the boys. Another crew planned to interview Mia. They wanted to weave in the viewpoint of one of the residents—and Mia had agreed to do it.

Olivia didn't want to get in the way of the action footage in the gym—she'd never forget wandering onto the court and interrupting that game the first day she came to the shelter.

She decided to watch them interview Mia. They'd set her up on the steps to the residence rooms. She looked great—not nervous. Olivia remembered how embarrassed Mia was when they first met. It was as if she didn't want anyone to know she lived at the center.

Now that she not only allowed herself to become a sort of media poster child for the homeless, couldn't she potentially catch the eye of her stepfather?

When Olivia recalled the comment she'd made about the "down-and-out," she blushed. While she still hadn't met too many people at the shelter, Mia and her mom were different.

The interviewer seemed distracted. He called out directions and even camera angles. He hardly connected with Mia, but she sat poised, waiting for his questions. At one point she looked up, saw Olivia, and winked.

Confusion reigned. The interviewer asked a question, and before Mia could get out an answer, he yelled, "Cut!"

"Don't worry," he said to Mia, "They'll piece it all together, and you'll hardly recognize it."

"Good thing," Mia said with a grin.

"So," the interviewer continued, "how does it feel to be homeless?"

Olivia couldn't believe how unfeeling this guy's questions were. If he were interviewing someone with a physical disability, would he focus on what they couldn't do? Olivia tried not to get too upset. She needed to keep her cool since she would be on soon.

Mia looked at the man for a long minute and then quietly began to speak. "I learned through this crisis the truth of the Bible verse 'For where your treasure is, there your heart will be also.' My treasure is here—my mother and my little brother—and friends like Olivia and Carter. My heart is full with that treasure."

"Perfect! Cut."

Bravo. Olivia caught Mia's eye and raised her hands to silently clap in a salute to her friend. She could see that many of those assembled were stunned by the simple truth Mia spoke.

Carter's segment finished as well. Mr. Jacobs, the producer, called for everyone to gather for the "surprise" scene.

Kinni McKay came out of Mrs. Bailey's office to join them. How Olivia wished Jane could have been there.

"Olivia O'Donnell," Kinni said directly to the camera, "you've been set up by your friends."

The camera panned across the semicircle of faces: Olivia's mom, Carter, Mia, Diane, Mrs. Bailey, and some of the kids.

"We've been told that no one here at The Shelter of His Wing—the women's shelter where you work—needs a makeover quite as much as you do." Kinni smiled and waited for Olivia to react.

Olivia rolled her eyes in mock disgust. "You guys don't like the way I look?"

The camera panned across her friends to get their teasing smiles.

Back to Kinni. "To soften this blow, I have a check here to help with an unforgettable shopping spree." She held up an oversized check with more zeros than Olivia had ever seen. "Are you ready to . . . change faces?"

Olivia smiled. "I'm game."

"Cut. OK. That's a wrap." The producer turned to another man. "I think we have plenty of interesting raw footage. I believe this one will be something special."

Kinni turned to Olivia and draped her arm across the girl's shoulders. "Strange, huh? It's hard for guests to see how we make a show out of this, but trust me, it all comes together."

"I look forward to it. My friend and I have been fans since the beginning."

"It's going to be fun to do you. I said that about you needing a makeover because that is what's scripted. It's what our audience expects, but you are lovely. Our makeup person is going to be delighted to see that smile of yours. In fact, the camera will love you."

Olivia didn't know what to say.

The producer came over and spoke to the group. "We need to pack it up, but thank you, everyone. Hope we didn't disrupt everything too much."

☆   ☆   ☆

When the last truck pulled out, they could finally relax. Olivia kept looking at Mia. She couldn't help wondering how Mia felt about the interview. There seemed to such a distinction made between a resident like Mia and a staff volunteer like Olivia.

Four short months ago, she thought, *I had the exact same attitude. Dear Father, please let this show come together right. Don't let it perpetuate that attitude. Let it shine Your light on the subject.*

As she climbed into the car with her mother, she had a feeling that they had a tough battle ahead of them.

12

Olivia opened her day planner to a blank page and began to make a list of things to do: "Organize closet and pack 'before' wardrobe for *CF*; do research paper; attend at least one of Tank's track meets; make sure transcripts received by colleges; organize snacks for next four youth group meetings; visit Diane."

She put down her pencil. She hadn't even begun to list the things she needed to do here at the shelter. *What am I going to do? I know I can ask Mom and Dad for help, but look at the list.*

What can they do? Mom might be able to do the transcript thing, and Dad would say that Tank would understand if I couldn't attend a meet, but . . .

She put her head down on the desk. *I'm so tired, and I feel as if I'm spinning my wheels.*

"Chip?"

She hadn't heard Carter come in.

"Are you OK?" He pulled up a chair, flipped it around so he could straddle the back, and positioned himself across the table from her.

"I'm just feeling a little overwhelmed. I had to start a whole new page because my to-do list outgrew the first one. I've barely made a dent on it."

"It's getting crazy, isn't it? Where's Mia?"

"She had an after-school appointment with her mom—a social worker or something."

"I worry because I think they are getting near their limit here," Carter said.

"What do you mean, 'limit'?"

"This is only a temporary facility until the families can move out to a place of their own. In order to en-courage that and to keep people from settling too deeply in this temporary spot, there's a time limit."

Olivia felt a cold, sinking feeling in her stomach. "But they are still in danger from Mia's stepfather. He may be looking for them."

"That's the way it is for a lot of families here. We teach them how to file for restraining orders against their abusers and how to be as safe as possible. It's sad, but it's reality for them." Carter sounded as if it caused him pain to think about it.

Mia forced to move? It seemed so unfair. "But I don't care about the other families here. I care about Mia." As soon as she said it, Olivia wished she could take it back. It was that old no-mercy thing rearing its ugly head again.

"Oh, Chip! I was just beginning to think I'd have to find a new nickname for you. I can see we still have a lot of work to do." Carter smiled that crinkly smile again.

Olivia wondered how he could be so easygoing and accepting. He never seemed to hold her shallow comments against her.

"Where were we when we got sidetracked?" he asked.

"I think I was talking about myself again and my overscheduled life." She held up the planner. "It must sound like a broken record."

"Let's see your list." He took the list and looked at it. "I'm right with you when it comes to the mountain of schoolwork. Why do teachers all seem to pile it on at the same time?"

"It's a conspiracy," Olivia said. "I didn't know you stressed about school stuff, too."

"I love being here at the center, and I tend to hang out here too much. I know I need to keep my grades up, but these guys are in such a tough transition time when they get here. I hate to miss out on the little time I have to influence them."

Olivia smiled. "You are right where God wants you, aren't you?"

"I wish that were totally true, but I know my first responsibility is to get my education." He made a face. "I sound like my father."

"Boy. And you teased me about my planner and my lists!"

"I always tease those I like best." He swung his chair around the table to sit alongside her so he could read her planner with her. "Let me help. What can we pick that we could cross off your list today?" He looked down the list. "Is your dad coming to pick you up tonight?"

"No. I'm taking BART."

"Well, how about I give you a ride out to the Javiers'? You can visit Diane, and I'll talk to Pastor Joe." He pulled out his wallet and looked inside. "I've got twenty-one dollars. Do you have a few more?"

"I have five."

"What do you think about ordering a pizza and bringing it over to them?"

"What a good idea. I'll need to call. I can't stay and eat without permission. One does not miss dinner at the O'Donnell house without a special dispensation."

Carter looked wistful. "Wow. That's great. We've got a housekeeper who sometimes puts something on the stove before she leaves, but my dad and I just bach it most of the time."

"Bach it?"

"Run the house like bachelors." Carter rubbed his hand across the table. "Before my mom got sick, she cooked every night. As far as we knew, the food magically appeared on the table."

Olivia sat still. Carter rarely talked about himself. She didn't want to break the stream of conversation.

"Those first couple years after she died, you'd find Dad still fumbling around with a box of macaroni and cheese a half hour before my bedtime." He gave a mock shudder. "We made it, though, and after his business began to turn some cash we were able to get help." He patted himself on the top of the head. "As you can see, missing a couple meals didn't stunt my growth."

"Let me see if I can reach my mom or dad."

"I'll go get my things. I think I'll call Pastor Joe and see what kind of pizza to get."

When Olivia finally reached her mom and told her what they planned to do, her mother said it would be OK.

"You'll get home in time to do that homework, right?" Mom asked.

"I will. Carter's loaded with homework, too," Olivia said.

"And to think they call your generation the slacker generation," Mom said with a laugh. "Give Diane my love. Tell her we're excited that the news is so hopeful, but that we're praying her through the treatment."

"I will."

Carter knocked on the doorframe before coming in. "What did your mom say?"

"She said pizza sounded like an excellent idea, and we inspired her to do the same menu at home. She said that I could be excused tonight." Olivia gathered her things together.

"Good thing, since I already ordered a large deep-dish pepperoni and olive pizza," Carter said.

"I take it you called Pastor Joe."

"Yup. Let's go before they give our pizza to somebody else."

✶   ✶   ✶

"It does my heart good to see Joe wolfing down that pizza with Carter." Diane ate lightly and moved back to the couch.

"Even though you couldn't eat a bite of it?" Olivia asked.

"If Joe ate what I have to eat, his belly button would soon be sticking to his backbone."

"No custard for him, eh?"

Diane laughed. Her skin had a pale look to it and she'd lost a lot of weight, but she said that was as expected. What she missed most, she told Olivia, was her hair.

"Chemotherapy attacks all the fast-growing cells," Diane explained. "That's how it zaps cancer cells. Problem is, those little chemo-kazis can't tell the difference between an enemy cancer cell and a friendly hair follicle."

"It will grow back, right?"

"Thank goodness. Can you imagine me being bald as a cue ball forever?" Diane rubbed a hand across her head.

"I don't know—it's more like a tennis ball." Olivia felt a little uncomfortable talking about the changes in Diane, but she followed Diane's lead. Teasing about it probably felt better than crying.

"Why the nausea and careful diet? Is that from the cancer?"

"No. The doctor thinks the cancer is long gone. It's actually from the cure. The cells in your mouth and stomach are also fast-growing cells, so they take a beating as well. It's temporary."

"It could have been a lot worse, couldn't it?" Olivia hated to even put words to what she'd been thinking.

"That's for sure. We never know what's in store for us, but if cancer was to be on my dance card, I'm thankful that we discovered it while it could be contained."

Diane looked over at Carter and Joe arm-wrestling for the last piece. "They never grow up, do they?"

"Your illness really affected Carter, you know."

"Joe and I suspected that might happen. We've been praying for him in that area." She wrapped herself up in the comforter. "OK, tell me how things are going."

"There's so much to do. I keep waking up in the middle of the night remembering yet another thing that needs to be done." Olivia's voice trembled a little. *Don't let me cry just because Diane asked.*

"You're talking about the center?" Diane asked.

"Yes. We need to get letters out to the businesses—I mean, the corporate donors who bought whole tables in the past."

"The letters from past years are in the computer. You updated the database already. You should just be able to change the basic letter—add the new information—and reprint."

"Mrs. Bailey showed me how to do that. We just need to decide on some of the specifics—like the theme —and I can merge the letters with the database."

"Great. When you get them printed, can you have someone bring them over here? I'll write a personal note on each one and do the stuffing and stamping." She stretched a languid arm up in the air, movie-star-like. "I'm a lady of leisure now, you know."

Olivia laughed. "Leisure? What's that?"

"Honestly? You don't really want to know. You'd go positively crazy lying around here hour after hour. That's why I'd really love to do some of that appeal writing."

"It would be great to include a handwritten appeal. I can see it now. Everyone's been so worried about you;

they'll be so happy to see your signature that they'll turn their pockets inside out."

Diane roared with laughter. "You, my sweet friend, have a larcenous side to you. Have you thought of becoming a professional fund-raiser?"

"In my spare time?" Olivia raised one eyebrow.

"Things are that bad?" Diane's face lost its teasing grin.

"It's not the shelter. I love working in the office there. It's everything all together. I sort of feel like I'm drowning." Olivia hadn't meant to burden her, but Diane had always been the one Olivia could talk to.

"Tell me what's been happening," Diane said.

"I'm loaded down with school stuff and falling behind—nothing critical yet, but that could change, especially since I'm going to be in L.A. for a full week. I'm barely keeping up with my family, and for church I'm doing nothing more than arranging snacks for youth group."

"Listen, Olivia, Joe is well aware that you've shouldered a good portion of my burden at the shelter. If you need him to give that job to someone else . . ."

"No. That's the least of my worries."

"Let me see your day planner."

Olivia opened it up to the current week.

"Yikes! No wonder. Let's see your famous goals."

Olivia flipped to those pages.

Diane ran her finger down the list. "How are you doing with Jane?" she asked as she put her finger on that goal.

"Terrible. I haven't had the time we used to have because of my job. Some misunderstandings arose, and there's just not enough time to work them out."

Diane's finger continued down the list. "What about the Aubrey thing?"

"It seems to escalate no matter what I do. As soon as I started working, she stepped into Jane's life. I know Jane needs friends, but every time I see them together, Aubrey looks at me in a weird, challenging way. I don't know . . ."

"What about your quiet time?"

Olivia stood up, closed her book, and laid it by her stuff. "Why does everyone keep bugging me about that? I know I need it, but I'm doing the best I can." She immediately felt guilty for snapping. "Can I get you something to drink, Diane?"

"Sure. I'll take some apple juice."

Olivia came back with the drinks. "Sorry for that, Diane. You might have guessed it's a sore spot."

"I got that feeling. The guys are playing around with that computer game. Do you have just a minute to pray with me?"

"Sure." Olivia sat down next to Diane. "Do you want to pray?"

"Why don't we each pray for the other?" Diane prayed for Olivia's crazy schedule, her list of to-do things, her relationship with Aubrey, and especially for Jane.

When it came time for Olivia to pray, she prayed for Pastor Joe and Diane and then for all the stuff they'd talked about—things like food sensitivity, too much lying-around time—she even prayed for Diane's hair.

"Now that's what I call specific prayer," Diane said when Olivia finished. "You gotta love a friend who prays for good hair for you."

Olivia laughed. "How I've missed you, Diane. You need to hurry and get better so you can come back."

"I'm trying," she said with a little punch to Olivia's arm. "While they play their game, I want to teach you a game I play. Mine's a mind game for dealing with stuff that makes you crazy."

"I need that."

"OK. Every time you start obsessing about something, you have to ask, 'What's the worst thing that can happen?'"

"I don't get it."

"Pick something you're worrying about."

"OK, the letters to corporate donors."

"If the letters don't get done this year, what's the worse thing that could happen?"

"The businessmen won't buy whole table tickets and our proceeds will be smaller."

"Let's examine that assumption. Some would call and get their tables, anyway—it's a tradition with them. And we could call closer to the event and pick up the other sponsorships. See? It would not be the end of the world.

"But take the worst-case scenario and say you're right," she continued. "That giving is affected because we couldn't get those letters out. Whose shelter is this, anyway? Don't we believe the Lord will provide the money?"

"Hmmm." Olivia had never considered not getting it all done. "It is interesting to try to picture the worst thing. I guess once you figure out how you'd deal with the worst thing, you don't worry as much."

"Bingo!" Diane snapped her fingers. "I'm not saying our work is not important, and I'm not encouraging you to shirk your job—that's just not in your blood. What I'm saying is that some things we consider earth-shaking really aren't."

"Sounds like a lesson you've recently learned, O Wise One," Olivia said.

"You'd better believe it, girlfriend."

Carter came into the room. "You ready to go, Chip?"

"Just about." She stood up and turned to Diane. "There was one more thing I wanted to discuss with you—the theme for this year's benefit. We can hammer things out over the phone, but let me just leave it with you so you can mull over it." Olivia paused. "I wondered if we could use one sweeping element for the theme of this year's benefit. What do you think about wings?"

"Wings?" Diane seemed to turn the word over.

"Because we are called The Shelter of His Wing, it seemed appropriate. And just picture the decorations the committee could create based on wings." Olivia began talking faster. "There are lots of songs that could tie in. And what do you think about coming up with a special recognition award for donors called the Angel Wing, because they are our angels and—"

"Whoa, Chip. Diane's head is going to start spinning in a 360-degree circle. Slow down."

Olivia laughed. "He's right. Don't get me on a roll."

"I love it," Diane said after a moment. "I positively love it. You, my friend, are a godsend." She laughed. "Have I ever told you that before?"

"Hmm, once or twice," Olivia said. "But I don't mind repetition."

"Please, Diane, stop, or I won't be able to get Chip's head in my car." Carter grabbed Olivia's hand. "Come. I promised to get you home in time for a hot date with Hamlet."

"Call me, and we'll talk." Diane waved them off.

135

Pastor Joe poked his head around the corner. "Thanks for the pizza. Next time, buddy, I get the last piece."

Carter only flexed his bicep and smiled like a little kid.

13

Here, Olivia. Put your bags right by the curb." Mom turned to kiss Dad and Tank. Olivia had a ton of luggage because she had to bring most of her closet so Kinni could critique it. Rip it to shreds, more than likely.

"Are you sure you don't want us to park and come inside with you?" Dad asked. Olivia could tell he hated to say good-bye.

"You can only come a few steps into the

terminal, anyway," Mom said. "They only let ticketed passengers past the security checkpoint now."

"We'll be fine, Dad," Olivia said as she gave him a kiss and a hug. "I love you."

"Get me either a Planet Hollywood T-shirt or a Mickey Mouse one," Tank said as he gave Olivia a playful punch in the arm.

"We'll talk later, Son, about your choice of icons. . . ." Dad turned to Mom. "Now you're sure someone will be there to pick you up?"

"Jack! They have a stretch limo picking us up, complete with camera crew. I think it's going to be a little hard to miss, don't you?" She gave him another hug.

"I still think we should be coming with you." Tank had tried to include himself from the moment he heard about the trip.

"You'd die if you had to wait in salons and spend days shopping for clothes." Olivia knew her brother would not last a single morning.

"Where are you headed, miss?" the skycap asked Olivia as he came over to get their bags.

"Los Angeles," Mom answered.

"You'll have a short flight today." He took their e-tickets and printed out their boarding passes and luggage tags. "First class. I've marked your bags priority."

"First class? No fair." Tank looked miserable. "Nobody told me she was going first-class," he complained to no one in particular.

"I'm going to get this curmudgeon in the car," Dad said. "Have a wonderful trip, girls. Call me."

They said their good-byes all over again until Dad finally pulled away from the curb.

"Here are your boarding passes and your luggage

claim tickets. I've stapled them into your envelope. You have extra luggage, but the up charge has already been paid." He handed the flight envelope to Olivia's mother. "Your gate is number seventy, right next to the Crab Pot. Your flight will begin boarding forty minutes before departure."

Olivia's mother handed him the tip, and they walked inside the terminal, trying to act like this was an everyday occurrence.

"I can't believe this is happening, Mom." Olivia held on to her mother's arm with both her hands for just one minute. "Will you pinch me?"

"I can't believe the difference in flying first-class. I may never be able to go back to coach again." Mom inhaled deeply as if she could breathe the rarefied air of first class clear out here in the terminal.

"But we haven't even boarded yet!" Olivia's cheeks practically hurt from smiling.

"Curbside check was enough to convince me."

As they made their way through security, their gate was the first one on the left. And then it wasn't long until they boarded their plane and were airborne. The skycap had been right. The flight would only be an hour long, but it didn't matter; they felt positively pampered the entire time.

When they landed at LAX, they were met by the producer and his film crew. Their fellow passengers stared as they deplaned and saw camera crews swarming Olivia. She could see them trying to figure out exactly *who* she was.

"Sometimes we get some great 'before' candid shots coming right off the plane," the producer explained.

Nice, thought Olivia. *Get 'em while they're groggy.*

One of the crew asked for their ticket folder and went to retrieve the luggage. The rest of the crew followed them to their limo, filming along the way.

As they got into the car, Olivia whispered to Mom, "I had no idea they made such a fuss over guests. None of this ever shows on the program."

"I'm not complaining," Mom said.

"I wish I had been able to talk to Jane before I left. I promised her I would, but there was no time, except to dash over and give her the research paper she promised to turn in for me while you waited in the car." Olivia did not want anything to ruin the trip for them—it was such a rare treat to be able to spend a whole week with Mom—but she still felt a nagging unease about Jane.

The chauffeur came back and showed them how to operate the windows, the air-conditioning, the music system, and the privacy panel. He opened the beverage area and told them they could either help themselves or pick up the intercom phone and ask him to pull over. He'd then be happy to come back here and serve them.

Mom looked like she would burst out in laughter at any moment, but she kept her hand over her mouth.

"And the telephone is right here. Please feel free to use it. If you want to dial international calls, dial zero-one-one first. All calls have already been authorized and paid for by your hosts as a part of the package, so feel free." He backed out of the doorway. "Enjoy your ride."

As he made his way to the driver's seat, Mom said, "I believe I may."

They both dissolved into giggles.

"Why not call Jane from the car?" Mom asked.

Olivia did not have to be told twice. She dialed the area code and number.

A voice answered she did not immediately recognize.

"Hello? Could you tell Miss Jane Broga this is Olivia O'Donnell calling from the backseat of a stretch limo?" She laughed.

"Jane went out to her car to get something." There was a definite chill in the voice.

"Aubrey?"

"Yeah? So?"

"It's Olivia."

"I already managed to get that."

"May I talk to Jane?"

"It's like I said, she's busy. Call back some other time." *Click.*

"That sounded one-sided." Mom took the phone from her hand and hung it up. "Don't let it rain on our parade."

"No. I won't."

"You know if you'd have talked to Jane, she would have been wild with excitement, right? I'll bet the 'brilliant's and 'fantastic's would have been flying."

Olivia knew Mom was right. Why let Aubrey do this to her? "OK, on to the Four Seasons in Beverly Hills, where we will rough it for the good part of a week."

"Would you care for a Perrier?" Mom asked with a straight face before they both dissolved into giggles.

The car pulled to a stop at the hotel. Their driver got out, but the hotel doorman came and opened the door of their limo. "Welcome to Beverly Hills and the Four Seasons."

"Thank you." Olivia's mom slid over and set her feet on the ground before gracefully standing.

That looked slick. Way to go, Mom. Now watch me fall out onto the stone. Splat. *This could make a great "before" shot.*

Somehow, though, Olivia managed to make it look as if she exited limos every day of her life. "Can you point out the direction of Rodeo Drive?" she asked the doorman. She wanted to be sure to walk Rodeo for Jane.

"It's only two blocks in that direction." The doorman pointed with his palm up and fingers together. "Left on Santa Monica, right on Rodeo Drive." It looked like he was offering it to her.

Must be the genteel way to point. No fingers jabbing in the air for him. Olivia made a mental note of the directions.

"You needn't walk, however," he intoned. "The hotel provides a complimentary limo for its guests. Simply call the concierge."

Olivia managed to swallow her whoop of delight. Their own limo driver, along with one of the bellmen, had been unloading luggage out of the trunk. "That will not be necessary," he said in honeyed tones. "The ladies have their own limo. It's at their service night and day."

Olivia looked at the two men. Each seemed to be pulling himself to new heights of ramrod posture. She couldn't help it. She had to look over at her mom. Yep, Mom got it as well—these two were trying to out-class each other. With each exchange about the luggage, the limo, the lobby—their accents became more polished and their attitudes more lofty.

She had to remember all this for Jane. How she hoped Jane would want to hear it all.

The lobby looked like something out of a Hollywood film. Gleaming floors of inlaid marble, lush plants, flower arrangements bigger than the size of their dining room table at home—it was simply overwhelming.

Once inside the lobby, their driver led them to a seating area. He explained that he was a celebrity escort. "We're contracted by studios or publishers to escort their guests to appearances. My job is to take care of you and to see that you have everything you need."

He had already registered them and double-checked their room. He handed them each a card that looked like a credit card. "There are your room keys. Your suite is on the sixteenth floor. Your bags have been placed in your room. One of the housekeepers will be up to un-pack your clothing, and the bellman will explain all the amenities to you."

"Thank you." Mom seemed a little unsure.

Olivia guessed what she was thinking: to tip or not to tip, that was the question.

"If you need me, use this cell phone. Simply press this button, and I'll find out where I can meet you or how I can serve you."

"Thank you." This time Mom smiled and began walking toward the elevators. She obviously decided not to tip.

Once the doors closed and they were alone, Mom let out a huge breath. "I had the terrible urge to say all right, already."

"It's a big responsibility, isn't it, having to provide work for all these people?" Olivia laughed as the doors slid open and they stepped out into the hall.

"There it is." Mom slid her card key into the lock and heard the click. "I'm getting the hang of who to tip and who not to tip. Hired by the studio: They take care of it. Part of the hotel: We—"

Olivia opened the door. "No way!"

Mom stepped inside behind her. "Get my camera. This is unbelievable."

The room consisted of a living room separated from the bedroom by double French doors. Olivia did the first walk-through while Mom stood in the center of the room trying to get a decent camera sweep.

"You're not going to believe this. There are two bathrooms. No, wait. There are two marble bathrooms with gold fixtures. This is like *Lifestyles of the Rich and Famous.*"

"I think you failed to mention the telephones and televisions in each bath," Mom said as she came up behind Olivia. "Just think, we could be taking a bath, talking to each other on the telephone."

"Mom. Can I try Jane just one more time? Then I'll stop thinking about her, and we can keep oohing and ahhing together."

"Sure." Mom gave her a little hug. "I know she's on your mind."

Olivia dialed the number and waited while it rang. "Drat. It's the answering machine." She waited until she heard the beep. "Hi, Jane, this is your good pal, O, dying to talk to you. You won't believe this, but I'm staying in a suite. We each have our own bathroom. In fact, I am calling you from the bathroom. Call me if your mom says it's OK." She gave the number. "When we graduate from college, we *have* to come here to stay, even if it's just for one night."

She turned to her mother. "How much does it cost for this room for one night?"

Mom walked over and looked at the back of the door where the prices are posted in fine print. "You don't want to know." She laughed. "It's eight hundred and twenty-five dollars per night."

"OK, Jane, so it's eight hundred and twenty-five dollars a night, but we have four-and-a-half years to save for it. Call me. I miss you. Call me."

"Couldn't reach her?"

"No, but there's nothing more I can do. At least she knows I was thinking of her. She'd love this place— she's crazy enough to want to hear every detail."

Olivia wondered why she didn't feel she needed to call Mia or Carter. *Interesting.* Mia would smile, but she'd probably be secretly horrified at the opulence and playacting.

And Carter? She could see him just taking this in stride. In fact, he and his dad probably stayed in places like this. He wouldn't be surprised, but he wouldn't be impressed either, she guessed. He always had other things on his mind—like his boys at the shelter.

The phone rang, and Olivia answered it. *Weird. I can't believe I'm still hanging out in the bathroom on the phone.*

"Olivia?"

"Yes."

"Welcome to Southern California. This is Michael Jacobs, *Changing Faces* producer. Are you ready to get to work?"

"I am."

"Great. You and your mom are free to relax, sight-see, or do dinner and a show tonight. Just let Philip know, and he'll arrange it all."

"Philip?"

"Your escort—your driver."

"Oh. Right."

"Tomorrow morning, we need you here at eight o'clock. We have a full day planned. We'll go over the week's schedule then. Will that work?"

"Sure."

"Philip will contact you to let you know what time to meet him in the lobby to get over to the studio on time. Any questions?"

"I'll save them all for tomorrow."

"Right. Tomorrow, then. Have fun tonight and then sleep well."

Later that night, as Olivia snuggled under her down comforter and nestled deeper into her goose feather pillow, it finally sank in—the adventure had well and truly begun.

Lights,
Camera, Action

14

Welcome, welcome, welcome."

Michael Jacobs met them at the door. Olivia recognized him from the session at the shelter. "We'll start the morning with a meeting. We want to get everyone on the same page." He carried a clipboard and a stack of papers. "Follow me."

Philip waved good-bye to them as he walked out to the limo, and they fell into step behind Michael. The studio wasn't as big as Olivia expected. She'd watched cameras run through hallways on David Letterman and thought all studios looked like that.

Michael led them into a glass-walled conference room and pulled out chairs to seat them before he sat down. The room was filled with people. "Good. Everyone's here." He paused. "This is Olivia O'Donnell and her mother, Patricia—Patty." He swept his hand toward those seated at the table. "Ladies, meet the team. You already know Kinni."

Kinni smiled. The welcome was warm and genuine.

"This is your fashion consultant, Maree Moore from *Spree* magazine."

Maree smiled and gave a tiny wave to Olivia. "Nice to meet you."

"Next is your hair team from Steef & Cole—stylist Steef Alton and colorist Jill Reyes."

"We're going to have fun together," Steef said. "Great hair. A little mousey, wouldn't you say, Jill?" He looked over at Jill. "But no question, you've got great texture."

Jill just mouthed a friendly "hi" to Olivia.

"And Bianca from Spa by the Sea is our skin and makeup consultant."

Bianca seemed to be studying Olivia. "She's lovely," she said to the team. "This will be a great episode."

"Our producer agrees. He's thinking of doing extra promotion for this episode because of the intriguing tie-in with the shelter. You know how some reality shows are doing celebrity shows? We're going in a totally different direction by focusing on a charity."

"Much of the B-roll was shot at the shelter," Kinni told the group. "We taped a knockout interview with one young girl that will make a fabulous trailer for the show."

148

"You're talking about Maria Elena?" Olivia asked.

"Yes. Wait until you see the edited version—simple yet powerful. The trailer is the commercial that promotes the show," Kinni explained.

"We want to make sure to include a stunning evening ensemble for Olivia, since the reveal will coincide with the shelter's annual benefit," Michael reminded them.

"Will you actually be there for the benefit?" Olivia asked Kinni.

"Yes, we'll have to film you there, surrounded by your friends."

Olivia's mind began to click. *Think like a real PR person. Think like Diane.* "Could we possibly promote you as a guest? I think it would be a huge draw in Bay Vista. Do you know how many *Changing Faces* fans you have there?"

Michael and Kinni exchanged grins before Michael spoke. "If anyone had a doubt that this high school student really *is* an assistant public relations director, banish that thought. I wish we'd had our PR people in here to hear that—she puts them to shame."

Everyone laughed, and Olivia blushed at the compliment.

"I think it's a great idea, Olivia," Kinni said. "I'd be happy to consider it an appearance, sign autographs, and help promote the shelter. It's a wonderful charity and, thank goodness, *Changing Faces* has not yet stooped to charging charities for our help. Besides, while we're shopping for your magical ball gown, I'll look for one of my own and put it on the company tab!"

Michael pushed the sheaf of papers toward the

team. "Take one of these, everybody. This is our schedule for the week. Look it over while I run the drill for Olivia and Patty."

Papers were passed around the table and everyone started marking them up.

"If you've watched the show, you may be surprised to find out that we do not necessarily do the segments in order. We film according to everyone's availability. So you may end up doing some shopping before we've done all the 'before' segments. The show is put together in the cutting room, and it will flow just as it should when it airs.

"Another question that sometimes comes up: Some guests have wondered why we don't set up salons and a fashion set right here in the studio. It would be a lot easier to bring the stylists here to do your hair and makeup or style your wardrobe. The reason we go out into the stores to shop and into the famous salons is because promotional consideration is given to those firms participating."

Olivia looked puzzled. "Promotional consideration?"

"Sorry," Michael said. "Sometimes I forget that we speak a weird language here. Let me explain. The reason we take the cameras into those stores and salons is that it helps promote those businesses—it's like advertising, only much better. In exchange for the promotion, those firms give us clothing, makeup, hair services for free. In fact, clothing designers and manufacturers send us more products than we could ever use, in the hopes that we will feature those designs on one of our shows." Michael smiled at her. "Did I make that clear at all?"

"Yes. What do you do with all those extra things?"

Olivia didn't know why this interested her so much, but as soon as he mentioned all those extra products, she felt a stirring—something about it really got her juices going. *Weird.*

"Everyone's still working on the schedule, including your mom. That's good. We all need to work out any potential bugs right now." He stood up and addressed the room. "You keep working. I'm going to show Olivia the vault."

"Oh, no, not the vault," said Steef in a funny falsetto.

"Ignore him and come on." Michael laughed and gestured toward the door. Down one of the side halls, he stopped at a room with double doors. He ran a card through the security lock and punched in a code on the keypad. "Here it is."

Olivia blinked as he switched on the lights. Here was a gigantic warehouse with dozens—no, maybe hundreds of racks of clothing—every color of the rainbow and every size. There were more shoes and boots than ten shoe stores could stock. On one wall ran shelves with row after row of wire baskets containing makeup and hair products. Clear drawers held delicate lingerie.

"Awesome! I've never seen anything like this," Olivia said. "What will you do at the end of the season with all these beautiful things?"

"We plan to develop some kind of systematic way to gift it to charity. We just haven't had time to get around to it."

Charity, huh? No wonder Olivia got that funny excited feeling when he mentioned the promotional clothing. *God,* she prayed silently, *sometimes You crack me up. But I get it—that was Your nudge. I recognize it now. I have no idea what You want me to do about it, but I'll try to listen.*

Olivia smiled. *OK, Lord, I need to listen especially hard since we haven't been getting together regularly. But I'm here, and that's a miracle in itself. This stuff is all here, and it's probably not a coincidence. As Pastor Joe would say, 'I'm all ears.'*

"You look a million miles away. I guess this is all overwhelming. I can already tell that you are going to have a great week." He stood back so she could leave. Then he closed and locked the door, resetting the code.

From that moment on, the week sped by. Olivia went through the painful "before" sessions when they said just about everything Jane ever said. Why Diane decided to send that photo of her in a tank top with flannel bottoms was something that would have to be dealt with later. Olivia couldn't help but smile to think about Diane picking ugly before-shots.

The clothing sessions with Kinni were more fun than she expected. Kinni really helped Olivia see that clothes could be practical and beautiful at the same time.

"You're an honor student in high school, plus you work a heavy schedule at the shelter," Kinni said to Olivia, cameras rolling all the time. "I'm guessing you have precious little time to fuss. Am I right?"

"If you only saw my schedule . . ." Olivia said.

"Let me give you three keys to looking great in active wear—cut, color, and fabric. Don't skimp on any of these. You can achieve a polish and still be comfortable and casual."

"I think I know what you mean." Olivia thought about that polish Aubrey always seemed to have. "I just don't know how to achieve it."

"Well, that's what we plan to teach you."

And then the lessons began. Kinni gave her guidelines for determining if the fit was right. "So many teens go for skintight, but all it does is give you wrinkled fabric while accentuating every one of your figure flaws." Kinni demonstrated this by pulling the fabric tight on Olivia's jeans. "Good fabric should be allowed some ease, a little flow. Let it skim your body, bending and curving in a supple motion." She demonstrated each one of those principles.

By the time she and Mom went shopping, Olivia understood so much more about fashion and fabric. She'd also spent plenty of time looking at her own body. The bad thing was that she knew every single flaw. The good thing was that she learned how to camouflage them and how to accentuate her best features.

Olivia's mom learned as well. Off-camera, the stylists offered her tips and helped her with shopping. Every night when mother and daughter arrived back at the hotel, they could do little more than drop into chairs and order room service. One thing they agreed on—they had never had such fun together.

☆   ☆   ☆

"This morning we'll hit three boutiques on Rodeo Drive to find your gown for the benefit," said Kinni soon after they walked into the studio on Thursday. "Most of your clothes shopping is finished, though we may do another shoe run this afternoon. Maree will come with us again."

"I can see that it will be another grueling day in Beverly Hills," Olivia said, trying to keep a straight face.

Kinni laughed. "How are you holding up, Patty?"

"Famously. We've had such fun this week." Mom smiled. "I had no idea how refreshing this break would be for me. It's been a long time since I focused on fun and craziness for any length of time."

"Mom is volunteer extraordinaire," said Olivia. "My frantic schedule is only rivaled by hers."

"I'm so glad to hear it's been fun," Kinni said. "For many of our guests, it's highly stressful. Satisfying in the end, though, according to all reports."

"We appreciate the mission behind this. I'm not forgetting why you chose me." Olivia's voice grew wistful. "I wish you could see the lives changed at the shelter. And even those who don't stay long enough to see big changes get a place of acceptance and safety for a time."

"You love that place, don't you?" Kinni asked.

Olivia pursed her lips and looked at Mom before answering. "It's funny you say that. Mom knows—I took this job kicking and screaming. I told anyone who'd listen that it definitely was not my thing. In fact, when Diane got sick, I had been planning to resign, but, you know . . ." She gave a soundless snort, as if enjoying a private joke. "You're right. I do love the shelter and its mission, and I'm coming to appreciate the people who live there."

Mom laughed. "And I'll bet no one is more surprised than you."

Kinni laughed as well. "I could have told you that when we visited." She changed the subject. "The shelter element is what makes this episode so special. It adds a layer that brings balance to what we do. And the producer is pulling out all the stops on this one."

"We're honored," said Mom.

"So," Olivia said, "we shop till we drop today, and then—"

"And then tomorrow is wrap day. You have hair and makeup in the morning, and in the afternoon you come back here for your on-camera fashion show and the still-model photography."

"That will be a full day," Mom said.

"That's why we have you fly home on Saturday morning. You do know that the reveal—that moment when we supposedly catch your friends and coworkers seeing you for the first time—takes place back in Bay Vista?"

"But it won't really be when they see the new me for the first time since the benefit's still almost three months away, right?"

"To the camera it will look like almost no time has elapsed, but you're right; there's a good piece of time in there." Kinni looked at her notes. "When we come, we bring the whole crew again for filming, but we add Steef to do your hair again and Bianca for your face." She paused. "I may bring Maree for fashion styling as well. We'll see."

Speaking of Maree, as soon as she arrived at the studio, they got into the limo and headed out to shop. The camera crew followed in a van, occasionally taking film of them getting in and out of the car or going in and coming out of a shop.

Olivia found the process interesting. When they got to a boutique, the film crew would shoot an outdoor shot making sure they got the façade and the sign and then a sweep of the interior. They usually got some shots of her shopping or with clothes draped over her arm. Next they'd go for the dressing room shots. She'd have to try on as many bad outfits as good, so Kinni could point out why something did not work.

Some of the bad ones made Olivia cringe. Hopefully the camera wouldn't dwell too long on those.

When they got to the shop where they actually planned to buy the gown, Kinni shopped with her so she could make the important fashion points. She had worked them out in advance and had them nearby on her clipboard in case she forgot.

"When you shop for that special dress—whether it is for a wedding, a prom, or a special event like The Shelter of His Wing annual benefit—you want to consider all the senses." She picked up a dress of sapphire blue silk taffeta. "Take this one. The striking jewel color would make Olivia distinctive in a room full of black."

"Black?" Olivia asked.

"A full three-fourths of the women at your event will play it safe and wear black. If you want to stand out in the crowd, add color."

She took the skirt in her hands. "This fabric is called tissue taffeta because of the rustle as it moves. Women of old understood what we've forgotten—use fabric that talks. Remember, satin whispers and taffeta rustles."

She took another gown—this time an ivory silk charmeuse. "Look at how this fabric catches the light. If you are slim, pick a fabric that's supple, that will flow like liquid over your curves."

She picked on one that had a beaded bodice. "And don't forget drama. Beaded and sequined gowns not only catch and reflect light, but many a fashion work of art is created in the encrusted look of exquisite beading." She put the dress down. ". . . And, cut."

"Wow. That was so interesting." Olivia had no idea so much went into fashion.

"Thanks. We work hard to teach as well as entertain."

Maree joined them again. "OK, are you ready to try on your ugly ones?"

"Sure. Let's get that out of the way." Olivia couldn't believe they'd find anything ugly in here. The place sparkled like the ballroom from the Cinderella story.

Once they filmed those dresses, Maree came over with a silk tissue taffeta gown of a pink-tinged ivory laid across her arms. "You don't want to know how much this gown costs. We're not adding the price into the total cost of your makeover—there's not enough money in the budget for it. We'll announce that the boutique donated it."

The cameras began to roll as Maree handed it to Kinni, who reverently shook out the voluminous skirt. The bodice was classic and plain—almost Audrey Hepburn-like in its simplicity.

"The color is beautiful. Perfect. Just the color of angels' wings." Olivia knew before even trying it on that it was meant for that evening. "Our theme is wings. . . ."

"Try it on, then," Kinni said. "You'll wear a little sparkly cashmere evening sweater over it."

Olivia tried it on. Maree and Kinni were right. It was perfect. It rustled when she moved, and the pale color shimmered under the lights of the dressing room. She slipped on the sweater.

"Exquisite. Absolutely perfect," Kinni said to the camera. "Olivia is still a girl, so the look of the tiny sweater and the innocence of the ivory taffeta couldn't be better. It creates an unforgettable look."

Olivia turned around. She could see Mom off

camera, smiling. Yes, this would be the dress she'd remember her whole life.

"All you need to set off your pale skin is a simple strand of pearls and a pair of pearl drop earrings." Kinni smiled. ". . . And, cut."

"You know how to get the pearls to wear that night, don't you?" Kinni asked when the camera moved away.

"Buy them?" Olivia had no idea.

"Good try, but you wouldn't want to have to pay for the kind of pearls I'm talking about—it would amount to at least a year of private college." Kinni dropped her voice. "You, being a public relations person, need to learn to enlist the help of everyone you can think of to your cause. It makes them feel good and connects them to your organization."

"I'm not following," Olivia said.

"Go to your local jewelry store and arrange to borrow their best pearls for the evening. Your jeweler will have insurance on them in case something happens. Tell him his pearls will appear on our program. Then you list him on the program as a sponsor."

"Kinni, you are amazing."

"Why, thank you for noticing," she said with a Southern accent.

Maree came over. "I think we're done here. I want to take Olivia over to get a pair of jeans, another sweater, and one or two new tops. Do you want to come, or do you want me to take the camera crew and let this be shopping-alone footage?"

"Let's go with that. I'll go back to the studio and script the wrap."

It's a **Wrap**

15

The next morning Philip took Olivia and Mom to the Steef & Cole Salon. Steef met her at the door. "Welcome. Come in."

After introducing her to some of the other stylists, he led her over to his chair and helped get her settled. "How do you normally wear your hair?" he asked.

"Honestly? Pulled back with a scrunchie like this." She smoothed her hair with her hands and pulled it into a low ponytail and slipped a scrunchie off her wrist onto her hair.

"Well, it's quick." The camera caught the

roll of his eyes. "How about if I give you a great style that's every bit as quick but frames your face and accents those gorgeous eyes?"

"Anyone who tells me I have gorgeous eyes can do anything he wants to my hair," Olivia teased.

He washed her hair off camera. The cameras rolled again briefly as he started cutting.

"A great cut will give you easy-care hair and a high-fashion look all at the same time." He snipped confidently, picking up a strand, bending it and knowing just how to angle the cut. "Because you are still a high school student, we don't want to get into coloring in a big way since color requires a fair amount of upkeep."

"Especially since my mother is not wild about me having colored hair."

"There is that," he said with a laugh. "Fortunately, your mother did agree to let us pop the color a little with delicate highlights, so as soon as I have you cut, we'll let our colorist, Jill, take over the weave."

When the color was done, she ended up back in Steef's chair. "The key to a crisp style is in the product we put into your damp hair. Since you have fine hair, we want to add body with a mousse." He squirted a mound of foam into his hand and worked it into her hair from the scalp to the ends. "Now, all we have to do is blow and go."

True to his word, he lightly blow-dried her hair, and it looked wonderful. The layering allowed it to frame her face. The shine and shape made all the difference.

"I love it," Olivia said as she turned first one way and then another in front of the mirror. "Even better, I know I can do this at home. Thank you."

". . . And cut," the cameraman said.

With her hair done, they climbed back into the limo for the ride to Spa by the Sea, where Olivia would have the facial makeover.

Philip chatted comfortably with them as he drove. Olivia remembered when they first met him almost a week ago. They expected him to drop them off at the hotel and return at the end of the week to deliver them back to the airport. Instead, he took meticulous care of them both day and evening—drove them to dinner, arranged theater tickets, managed to get them into the taping of a new sitcom pilot, made sure they stayed on schedule, and a hundred other little things. Like so many others she'd met this week, he'd become a friend.

After days of wheedling, Olivia finally convinced him to accompany the team to Bay Vista for the benefit. He said he'd have to drive up early to have the limo available. Mom promised to cook him the best home-cooked meal he'd ever eaten. It was probably the meal that sealed the deal.

As the car pulled up in front of the salon, Olivia could smell salt in the air. "Is the beach near here?"

"Just about a block over," Philip answered.

"I can't believe we've been in Southern California almost a week and have not made it once to the beach."

"It couldn't be because we were a little busy, could it?" Mom asked.

"How did the time slip by so quickly? I so wanted to check out the secondhand shops on Melrose Avenue." Olivia stood on tiptoes, trying to see over the rooftops to see if she could catch the tiniest sliver of water. "If only we had a little more time . . ." They stood there and waited for the camera crew to catch up with them for the façade shots, listening to the sound of gulls.

"There will be other times," Mom promised. "Not that we'll enjoy this level of luxury. But, hey, we've done it the rich-and-famous way; next time we'll try the obscure, innovative, on-a-shoestring kind of trip."

"Good idea. And secondhand shopping will fit right in," Olivia said.

"OK. They're done with the exterior," Philip said. "Let's go inside."

"Welcome to Spa by the Sea," Bianca said as they walked into the spa. The interior designer had borrowed the colors of the ocean. Cool blues and sea greens mixed with sand, but the predominant color was white.

"Do you feel the cooling breezes off the ocean?" Bianca asked. "I'm going to show you how you can achieve that freshness in your facial care."

"I'm ready." It sounded so good to Olivia.

Bianca began with a cleansing routine. "This should only take about two minutes each morning." She smoothed on a cleanser that she applied with a defoliating pad. After rinsing it off, she used a cooling splash. "And about once a week, when you have a little extra time, you can do a deep-cleansing mask."

Olivia couldn't answer. Bianca stood behind her, massaging little circles into Olivia's face. She'd be snoring if Bianca kept it up much longer. *Ahhhhh.*

After the segment on skin care, Bianca picked up a pair of tweezers, holding them up and talking to the camera. "We need to refine the shape of your brows. We want to open up the eye area, still keeping a full enough brow to frame your gorgeous eyes. Make sure not to overpluck—it's a common problem these days, and it leaves a woman with a vacant expression."

Olivia steeled herself against flinching every time the tweezers came near her face. *Good thing they don't film the actual torture.*

"Your skin is excellent. We won't need to use any foundation other than a tinted moisturizer with a light dusting of translucent powder." She smoothed the moisturizer on, followed by the powder.

"Your eyes may be your best feature. The color is wonderful—a true hazel. Sometimes they're mistaken for green, sometimes brown." She took out a set of brushes and lined them up on her counter. "We'll give you a wide-eyed look with a mocha frost and a smudged espresso eyeliner. And then we'll go deep black with the mascara to bring out the drama in your eyes." Olivia sat facing Bianca with her back to the mirror so she couldn't see the effect.

"We'll apply a light dusting of a rosy blush to the apples of your cheeks to give you a glow." Bianca continued to give a running commentary to the camera as she worked, brushing each cheek with a feathery touch of color.

"And for your lips, all you're going to want to do is apply a touch of clear lip shine. Your natural color is still perfect without adding any pigment." Bianca applied the gloss.

"There," she said as she turned the chair around. "What do you think?"

Olivia looked into the mirror. "Wow! It looks like me, only much better. I look healthier and more vibrant, don't I?"

"And that's what good makeup is supposed to do.

We call it *Changing Faces,* but in reality, we only enhance the one God gave you."

The cameraman raised his hand in the air. As he let it down, he said, ". . . And cut."

☆   ☆   ☆

"OK, ladies," Philip said as he held the car door open for them. "One more stop and we will really call it a wrap." As he helped Olivia in, he said, "And you, little darlin', look positively ravishing."

Olivia laughed. "I do believe you are paid to say that, Philip."

"No amount of money could induce me to say that if it weren't true. My mama taught me better."

As he went around to get into the driver seat, Mom whispered, "He's come a long way from his high-tone accent that first day."

Olivia agreed.

One last time to pull up in front of the studio. As Olivia walked in, Kinni came over to inspect her hair and makeup. "Perfect," she declared. "I knew we could count on Steef and Bianca. Oh, this is going to be an unforgettable episode."

Michael turned to the team. "Let's go, gang. It's time to play dress up." He put his arm around Olivia. "After this afternoon, the next time we'll see Cinderella will be at the ball."

The afternoon turned out to be the toughest of all. Changing outfit after outfit without wiping off her face or mussing her hair took real talent. Then lots of filming, followed by undressing and starting over again.

When they finally declared it a wrap, she flopped

into the nearest chair. "Nobody told me I needed to be in training for this."

"You sit," Maree said. "Patty, you too. I'll gather up the clothes and pack everything for you."

"And I'll take it all out to the car and call you when we're ready to head back to the Four Seasons," Philip said.

"Oh, I don't even want to think about going back to the real world." Mom sat slumped in a club chair with limp arms draped over the sides.

"I keep forgetting, Mom," Olivia said. "Do we have room service at home?"

"If only . . ."

16

Hello, Jane? It's Olivia. I'm ba-ack."
Jane did not reply. The silence on the other end of the phone seemed to last far beyond comfortable until she said, "That's right, you were gone."

Olivia tried to ignore the chill in her voice. "Did you get my message?"

"I got part of a message, but Aubrey re-played my messages for me and accidentally erased it."

"Oh." Olivia didn't know what to say. "I

wondered if you wanted to come over and talk. Do you have time?"

"I'd like to . . ." She must have covered the receiver. Olivia heard muffled sounds. "It's just not going to work out right now. Gotta bounce. Maybe later?"

"OK. Later."

Olivia looked at the phone before hanging up. *Hadn't Jane said she wanted to hear every single detail? And she had to "bounce"? Where did she pick up that word?* Olivia gave herself a mental shake and made a conscious decision not to dwell on it.

She flopped on the bed and opened her day planner. She was hopelessly behind. *How will I ever work in all the homework I missed? At least I had Jane turn in my research assignment in Brenner's class.* Mrs. Brenner accepted no excuses for late assignments. Even when people had a legitimate reason, she docked you a grade point for every day the assignment was late.

Olivia opened to a new page and titled it "Schedule." She set to work on a new plan that allowed her thirty minutes each morning for "personal grooming." She penciled in two hours a week for "clothing maintenance." That gave her time to do the laundry, give herself a facial, and do some homework. Multitasking would help her accomplish all she needed to.

The benefit needed to be moved to the top of her to-do list. Crunch time loomed, and the work needed to be meticulously scheduled—right down to the day. And what was that idea that began kicking around in her head in L.A.? Once she had a day or two to debrief and get some rest, she needed to get together with Diane and do a creative brainstorm.

She shut her day planner. *I need to get to bed. I'm*

beyond tired. Tomorrow I need to concentrate on church, homework, and youth group.

She looked at her rumpled bed with the worn bedspread. *Where's the down comforter and goose feather pillow when you need them?*

✿   ✿   ✿

"Chip! How we missed you last week." Carter came over to Olivia the moment she stepped into the room for youth group. "I can't wait to hear how things went in L.A."

"I should have brought my photos," Olivia said as Aubrey came up. Jane hung back, turning to talk to a freshman guy near the door. He looked surprised by her attention.

"Well, we all know a picture is worth a thousand words, so we'll wait for the pictures," Aubrey said as she slipped her arm into Carter's.

To his credit, Carter seemed surprised by her possessive gesture. He looked down at his arm and took a step away. The movement was automatic, but Aubrey acted like she'd been struck. She dropped her arm to her side.

"I've signed my guys up for a junior basketball tourney," Carter said to Olivia. "The excitement raised the noise level in the gym at least ten decibels higher during practice."

"How cool is that? How do you plan to deal with the ever-changing roster?" Olivia knew how temporary these kids could be.

"I talked to the city—they sponsor the tournament —and they decided to make an exception to their closed roster ruling."

"Super. I'll bet—"

"All you ever do is talk shop," Aubrey whined. "What's a girl got to do to get a little attention here?" She lowered her eyes and wound a tendril of hair around her finger.

"What needs attending?" Carter looked at her with a puzzled look.

Why doesn't she just go away? Olivia could see that Carter wanted to fill her in about the shelter, and she had so much she wanted to tell, but as long as Aubrey felt left out of the conversation, it was a lost cause.

"So, Aubrey, what happened while I was away?" Ignoring her was out of the question when she stood three feet away, so Olivia decided to try to include her.

"You were away?" she asked, opening her eyes even wider.

At that moment, Diane walked in the door. She wore a colorful scarf wrapped around her head, great earrings, and a wide-brimmed hat. She looked fragile, but Olivia longed to throw her arms around her, anyway. "Excuse me," she said as she left them to go see Diane.

"You look wonderful, Olivia!" Diane pointedly looked her up and down. She made her put her arms out to the side and pirouette. "If that's what a *Changing Faces* makeover looks like, sign me up."

Olivia got that funny prickle again. *Talk louder, God. I feel You nudging, but I'm not sure what You want.*

"I've never been happier to see someone walk through that door, Diane," Olivia said. "You are beautiful just the way you are. I almost feel like crying, seeing you standing there."

"Me, too." Carter had come up behind Olivia. "If you knew how much we prayed . . ." His voice caught.

"I felt it, Carter. Sometimes it felt like a blanket of love surrounding me. You will never know how much your faithfulness helped."

"Let's all get together again," Carter said. "I need to lose an arm-wrestling match so your good husband can get that piece of pizza I owe him."

Olivia laughed and looked to see if Pastor Joe heard. Directly in her line of sight stood Aubrey with her hands possessively on Jane's arm, talking fast and furious right into her face.

Isn't there anything I can do to stop this strange competition thing? It's getting impossible to ignore her.

Pastor Joe called for them to gather. As Carter sat down next to Olivia, he said, "If I give you a ride home, will you show me those photos?"

"Sure." Amid all the weirdness with Aubrey and Jane, her stomach felt lighter somehow.

"You look wonderful, Chip," he whispered. "I was afraid you'd come back looking way different—sort of made-up."

Olivia had never thought much about her looks, but tonight she felt sure she looked good. At least in one friend's eyes.

☆   ☆   ☆

Olivia stood in the line at the snack bar. All she wanted was to get a salad and join Jane at the senior bench where they'd hung out whenever they could this year.

Nearly every person she saw stopped her to tell her how great she looked. She'd worn a red ribbed sweater and the jeans Maree picked for her with a pair of sassy red Converse.

She had managed to blow-dry her hair and complete her makeup routine in just under the allotted time this morning. *It's all going to work out.*

She carried her salad over to the bench. "Hi, guys. Got any room for me?"

No one even looked up or stopped talking. What kind of game was this, anyway?

She felt humiliated and didn't know how to gracefully make an exit. Several small groups of people stood around and watched.

"We're over here, Chip." Carter waved his hand from the steps of the gym, as if Olivia had been looking for him. Mia was with him.

Olivia hurried over there. Having someone call to her took the sting out of Jane's rejection. OK, the sting remained, but it helped her keep a few shreds of pride.

"Carter and Mia, you are the best," she said when she slid in next to Mia. "I know you saw that whole thing."

"I don't get it," Mia said. "I thought you and Jane mended your friendship that day over hot chocolate."

"So did I. Maybe it's because I've been so busy and haven't had a lot of time to spend with her." Olivia racked her brain to try to figure out what could be wrong.

"I'm not buying that." Carter sounded confused. "A true friend doesn't play those kinds of on-again, off-again games." He propped his elbow on the table and leaned his chin into his hand. "Jane has been your friend since kindergarten, right?"

"Yes. It doesn't make sense. Jane's not like this."

"I'm not sensing this is about Jane," Mia said. "If you watch, she's not the one responding. She's just hanging back and letting Aubrey call the shots."

"It always boils down to Aubrey. Will you guys pray for me? Something's got to give." Olivia felt worn out. "I need to get going. I got a cryptic note from Mrs. Brenner that she wanted to meet with me during the last ten minutes of lunch."

"What's that about?" Carter asked.

"I don't know. It seems strange, doesn't it?" Olivia said.

"Maybe Carter and I can find a quiet place and take a minute to pray for you before we go to class," Mia said.

How Mia had grown in her faith.

Olivia stood to leave. She had the urge to hug them both before she left but put it down to being overly tired. Wouldn't that look even weirder? It would give Jane and Aubrey something else to snicker about.

✶   ✶   ✶

"Olivia. Good. Come in and sit down." Mrs. Brenner pointed to a chair across the desk from her.

"I got your note." Olivia sat down and dropped her backpack beside the chair.

"Frankly, I should not have asked to speak to you. I try to apply the rules fairly across the board. A rule is a rule, and when you neglected to make arrangements to turn in your research paper, I should have simply marked the *F* in the grade file and let it go at that."

Olivia sat frozen. *What was Mrs. Brenner talking about?*

"I'm new to Bay Vista, but from the first day I heard about you. You are well-respected and well-liked. The teachers talk a lot about the three-way tie for valedictorian."

Olivia was completely lost.

"That's why, when you flunked this assignment—"

"What do you mean, 'flunked this assignment'?" Olivia's chest hurt. Could a person have a heart attack at the age of seventeen?

"Olivia O'Donnell, did you think you could just coast on your past performance? I know you were going out of town, but you should have made arrangements—"

"I did. I gave my paper to Jane to turn in for me. She had it three days before I left and promised—" Olivia couldn't take it anymore. Her chest began to heave as she took deep breaths and tried to stem the tears. There would be no stopping this torrent. She laid her head on her arms across Mrs. Brenner's desk and hid her sobbing.

"Wait, Olivia. Please. There must be something—"

Olivia wished she could somehow be magically transported to her bedroom. She wanted to crawl under the covers and never come out. She hated dramatics— hated that she sat here in a classroom sobbing her eyes out, but she couldn't stop.

"Olivia, come. The bell's going to ring and fifth period will begin."

Olivia took a deep breath and looked up at the clock. Mrs. Brenner came around the desk and helped her up.

"Come. We'll go to your counselor's office."

Mrs. Brenner grabbed Olivia's backpack and led her through the back hall and teacher's lounge to the counseling office. On the way in, Mrs. Brenner called to the secretary, "Can you get one of student teachers to start my class?"

The office was empty, so Mrs. Brenner sat down

across the desk from Olivia. "Am I ever glad I decided to talk to you before giving you the grade that would have automatically knocked you out of running for valedictorian." She took a deep breath. "Can you tell me what this is all about?"

"I wish I c-could," Olivia said, trying to get her breathing to even out. "I can't seem to keep it all together this year, no matter how carefully I plan out my life." Olivia opened her backpack and pulled her day planner out and laid it none too gently on the desk. She opened to February. "Look at this." She turned to the goals pages, scratched out, written over, underlined, and notated. "And this."

Mrs. Brenner took the book from her hand and looked at it.

"I just can't do it anymore." The tears started flowing again.

"It's no wonder you can't do it," Mrs. Brenner said. "No one could keep up with this schedule. I can't believe you've continued to keep your grades up."

Olivia just shook her head. She felt completely empty. Why hadn't Jane turned in the paper?

"May I get personal with you?" Mrs. Brenner lowered her voice and turned the day planner toward Olivia. "This first goal." She pointed toward the goal to spend regular time with God. "Have you fulfilled this goal?"

That startled Olivia out of her circular thoughts. Not Mrs. Brenner, too. Was everyone she knew working together to gang up on her? "Well, I—I—"

"Please, don't get me wrong. It's none of my business, of course, but I just know that I couldn't get through a single day if I didn't start with prayer." She

175

smiled. "I guess I'm really not supposed to say that in this setting, and I'm not pressuring you in any way—the Lord knows you have enough of that."

"No. I appreciate you saying something. I meant to make it a priority, but the crazier stuff gets—"

"How well I know that," her teacher said. "When you said you 'can't do it anymore,' I may not have known what you need, but I know *Who* you need."

"You are right. I've managed to work in the new beauty routine we devised during my makeover. See there on my revised schedule?" Olivia pointed to the newest schedule. "Surely I can make time for my quiet time."

"I'm glad I decided to speak with you. I need to get back to my class," she said. "I'm going to speak to Jane Broga this afternoon and get to the bottom of this. I may want us all to meet tomorrow."

"Thank you, Mrs. Brenner."

"Stay as long as you like in here before going back to class."

Olivia did stay. She knew she looked a mess from crying. *Here I spent a whole week getting the ultimate beauty makeover. What I really need is a soul-deep make-over, Lord. Help me to be still and know that You are God— that You are Lord of my life. Otherwise, I cannot make it through. Today showed me that.*

She thought about Carter and Mia praying for her. And having her teacher talk to her about spending time with God. *Sometimes You really crack me up, God. First, Pastor Joe, then Dad, then Diane, now Mrs. Brenner—it's beginning to sound like a broken record.* She finally smiled. *Not that I'm complaining that You want to spend time with me, Lord. Precious few people seem to want my company lately, but when the God of the Universe keeps nudging me to have a visit with Him—*

Olivia sat quietly for a time. *I've done everything I know how to do, Father, to make a habit of spending time with You, and it keeps getting pushed to the side—not because I don't love You. I do. Will You do it for me? Give me a hunger for You so that I cannot even start my day without You. Rather than having me write it in my planner again, will You write it on my heart?*

"I'm sorry, Olivia. I ran into Mrs. Brenner, but I didn't know you were still here." Her counselor came in and sat down. "Do you need to talk?"

"No. I just needed more time to collect my thoughts. Now I think I need to repair my face before I get back to class."

In the restroom, as she blotted off the tear damage, Olivia felt lighter somehow. *You and me, God . . .*

Olivia finished her makeup routine with the last touch of lip gloss. Kinni had said she'd feel more able to tackle each day if she gave a few minutes to her grooming regimen. Kinni was right. She did feel ready.

What made her feel even more ready was the slip of paper in the pocket of her jeans. She pulled it out and read, "I sought the Lord, and he answered me; he delivered me from all my fears. Those who look to him are radiant; their faces are never covered with shame. Psalm 34:4–5."

See. I look radiant. She laughed to herself. If only Kinni knew—it *was* all about *Changing Faces*—just not the way she thought. *I needed to change to the radiant face that only comes from seeking God.*

Last night, Olivia had sat on her bed, replaying Mrs. Brenner's words. And it wasn't just her teacher who had talked to her about keeping a quiet time. None of those people—Dad, Pastor Joe, Diane, Mrs. Brenner—normally gave that kind of advice. *It took me long enough to get the message.*

She knew she'd turned a corner when she asked God to give her a hunger for Him. Pastor Joe had once told them that it's a prayer God will always answer. Her dilemma remained the same: How would she reinvent her schedule to make room for God?

As she looked over her revised, revised, revised schedule, it came to her. At this crazy stage in her life, room to carve out a regular quiet time simply did not exist. *Why not reinvent quiet time? What I need is a kind of quiet time on the run.* Bingo! Olivia knew this was God's answer to her. She'd long ago gotten into the habit of praying right in the middle of her craziness—why not this?

She borrowed a dozen colored index cards from her mom and cut them in half. Taking colored gel pens, she wrote the verses from each day of her devotional book—one per card. *If I can't get to the whole devotional, I know I can meditate on the verse several times throughout the day.* She thought about that God-hunger. Instead of a big meal, she could take smaller, more frequent meals—just a little taste of God's Word when time allowed throughout the day.

For today's verse—the radiant face one—she added

one of Jane's little peel 'n' stick happy-face stickers to the back. It seemed perfect.

Jane. What could Olivia do to get to the bottom of this weirdness? *God, please fix all this. If it's my fault, let me see what to do.*

✿   ✿   ✿

Olivia arrived at school forty-five minutes early. Mrs. Brenner had called last night to schedule a meeting with Aubrey, Jane, and Olivia.

Olivia put her hand over her jeans pocket. She felt more ready to tackle things today. When she walked into the meeting room, she was surprised to see not only Jane and Aubrey seated around the conference table but Aubrey's mother as well. Olivia sat down in the empty chair next to Mrs. Brenner.

"I spoke to each one of you girls yesterday, so you know why I called this meeting," Mrs. Brenner said. "Mrs. Ainsley, I'm surprised to see you here, but, of course, you are welcome to attend."

Jane hung her head and fiddled with her earring. Olivia recognized the signs of embarrassment in her friend.

Olivia tried to avoid eye contact with Aubrey, but a glance told her that Aubrey had been crying. Her eyes seemed puffy, and the extra makeup around them appeared smudged.

"When I looked into the disappearance of Olivia's research paper, so many interpersonal relationship problems came up that I felt we needed to talk," Mrs. Brenner said.

Mrs. Ainsley jumped right in. "I already told Aubrey

she was awful, plain awful, and I was ashamed of her."
She kept patting her hair, smoothing her skirt, and talking fast. Olivia remembered her from their earliest years of school. If Olivia's mom could not go on a field trip, Olivia always ended up with Mrs. Ainsley, walking beside her, holding her hand, listening to her talk in that nervous way while Aubrey ran up ahead with friends.

"Mrs. Ainsley, this is not about who is at fault as much as it is to sort through the underlying problem." Mrs. Brenner seemed surprised at Aubrey's mom's comment.

"This *is* about the underlying problem," Mrs. Ainsley continued. "Ever since Aubrey first started school, I kept telling her she needed to be more like Olivia. Aubrey always just wanted to play and have fun and—"

"Mrs. Ainsley! Aubrey and Olivia have two different types of personalities. Aubrey could never be like Olivia—"

"I know, and it broke my heart. I always hoped she'd go for top honors and all."

Olivia looked over at Aubrey. Tears ran down her face. *Please, Mrs. Brenner, do something.*

"Mrs. Ainsley, could you step out for a minute? I want to deal with the problem at hand with the three girls first. After that, I'd like you to meet alone with me, and then you, Aubrey, and I will meet. Would you please take a chair in the office? Ask the secretary to get you a cup of coffee. She'll be happy to do it."

Mrs. Ainsley seemed reluctant to leave, but she pushed back her chair and stood up without once looking at Aubrey. As the door closed behind her, the room grew silent except for the breathy sounds of Aubrey's solitary misery.

"I think I understand the history that led up to this incident. See if I have it right." Mrs. Brenner paused. "Aubrey, you've heard about how wonderful Olivia is for years, right?"

Aubrey didn't make eye contact but nodded yes.

"I'm guessing that's enough to grow a big case of resentment, isn't it?"

Aubrey did not answer.

"Jane, you and Olivia have been friends since kindergarten, right?" Mrs. Brenner asked.

"Best friends," Jane replied.

"And this year, when Olivia no longer had time, you and Aubrey started doing things together."

"That's right," Jane said. "At first, I did it to spite Olivia because I felt left out of her life. And I knew she and Aubrey always had this competition thing going."

Aubrey took a deep ragged breath. Olivia had never seen her so raw. As Aubrey raised her hands to her face, Olivia caught sight of her charm bracelets. *I wonder if that's why—each one of those charms represents someone who chose Aubrey—sometimes someone who chose Aubrey over me?*

Stop it! Let it go. Aubrey is poison. If you go getting sentimental, you will get cut off at the knees again. Olivia straightened her back and folded her arms across her chest.

Jane continued. "As I got to know Aubrey, I liked her for herself. She's different from Olivia, of course, but she's so much fun, and she loves people. They flock around her, and she can't help but entertain them."

Aubrey looked up in surprise.

"You liked me even though you knew everything was about Olivia?" Aubrey said.

"I still like you. This Aubrey-Olivia competition has always been beyond understanding, but once I got to know you, I liked you."

Aubrey looked down at her hands, then looked up at Jane again.

"So to continue," Mrs. Brenner said, "Jane and Olivia have maintained their relationship as best they can this year, and Olivia gave Jane her research paper to turn in on the appropriate day. Right?"

Both Jane and Olivia nodded.

"And on that day, Jane got called out of class early to see the counselor, so she put Olivia's paper on Aubrey's desk, asking her to turn it in. Am I still right?"

This time Jane and Aubrey nodded.

"And what happened when it came time to turn it in, Aubrey?"

"I j–just couldn't do it. Every time I thought of Olivia sitting on the podium as valedictorian, it made my skin crawl. I knew my whole graduation would be filled with Mom telling me if I'd worked harder like Olivia, I could have been up there." She started crying even harder. "I opened my folder and just slipped her paper behind my notes and left with it." Aubrey looked at Olivia and sighed. "I should have known Olivia would come out on top again."

"What do you mean?" Mrs. Brenner asked.

"I mean, my mother still thinks Olivia walks on water, but instead of seeing me only as a disappointment, she now believes I'm evil for doing this." Aubrey clasped her hands and pressed her fist against her mouth.

Jane continued for her. "Aubrey found out about *Changing Faces*. When Olivia called from L.A., it seemed to be the last straw for Aubrey. Because she had always 'won'"—Jane made the gesture of quote marks in the air—"when it came to style and appearance, she hated the thought of Olivia doing the makeover thing."

Aubrey spoke up. "I mean Olivia has grades, brains, friends—including Jane for a best friend—all the teachers love her, and she may even have the best guy in school. It was so unfair that she won the lottery on top of all that."

"I don't understand—the lottery?"

"Well, not literally, but how many girls will ever get a chance to win a Hollywood makeover, ride in a limousine all week, stay in the Four Seasons . . . ?"

"How do you know so much about my trip?" Olivia didn't mean to address Aubrey, but she was puzzled. When she had called Jane, Aubrey hung up so quickly; she couldn't have heard all that.

"The whole thing chewed on Aubrey," Jane said. "She spent hours online, looking at your hotel, imagining every detail of your trip."

"I know. I know. Jane keeps telling me I'm obsessed, but—"

"But what?" Mrs. Brenner's voice sounded sad.

"I don't know how to stop being jealous," Aubrey said, spreading her fingers wide as she gestured in the air.

"Jealous? That's ridiculous," Olivia said. "A crowd of people follow you wherever you go. You have guys at the snap of a finger. When I tried to describe the kind of look I hoped to achieve in my makeover, your polish and fashion sense is the one I described." *Leave it alone, Olivia.*

"But my mom always wanted me to be you."

"I want to talk to your mom afterward," Mrs. Brenner said. "I'm guessing she was just trying to spur you on by holding Olivia up to you. I'll bet she never wanted to wound you."

Aubrey didn't say anything.

Mrs. Brenner picked up the phone on the desk. "Can you ask Miss Garcia to start my first period class? I'll be tied up a little while longer. Tell her the plans are on my blotter." She paused to listen. "Thanks."

"Here's what we are going to do. I suggest Jane and Olivia go somewhere and talk things out. Aubrey gave me your paper, Olivia. I'll not dock any points because of the circumstances." She stopped and wrote out a pass. "Jane, you and Olivia spend first period on the senior bench talking this out. Here's a pass—you'll be missing my class, so consider it excused."

"Aubrey, can you wait outside while I talk to your mother? Afterward, I want to talk to you both. We're going to handle this whole incident between us. I've decided not to take it up with the dean." She took a slow breath. "I think this may be a turning point for all three of you."

✿   ✿   ✿

Jane and Olivia walked out toward the senior bench.

"I can't believe what a mess this has been," Jane said. Her usual enthusiasm was missing.

"I know, and it's not just Aubrey," Olivia said.

"That's right, I was at fault as well." Jane sat down.

"No. That's not what I meant." Olivia leaned over to let her backpack slide off her arm before sitting down.

"I was thinking of the way I abandoned our friendship this year."

"OK, then me first." Jane turned so she could look at Olivia. "I missed you. It seemed like every time I wanted to call you, you were at the shelter or somewhere else. I got tired of running after you like a puppy."

"It was never like that, was it?" Olivia couldn't believe Jane felt that way about their friendship.

"I don't know. I didn't recognize the resentment building. When I started hanging around with Aubrey, at first I felt very uncomfortable with her constant talk about you."

Jane shifted. "Pretty soon, I stopped trying to stand up for you. I just let her go on about you, especially while you were away. I didn't realize how damaging it is to listen to that stuff. You don't even have to agree or say anything. Listening is enough to subtly change you."

Olivia sat listening.

"Will you forgive me for letting resentment into our friendship?" Jane asked.

"Of course. I so understand, and I've felt awful about all this. When I was in L.A. all I could think about was you. I've missed you so much. But how do we get back our old friendship?"

"I've thought a lot about this. I'm not sure we can ever get it back the way it was," Jane said.

"What do you mean?" Olivia felt the start of tears. Jane didn't want to restore their friendship?

"As we grow up, our lives change like yours did this year. I mean, what if we go to different colleges? What about when one of us gets married and the other is still single?"

"You are thinking way ahead."

"We need to have the kind of friendship that can withstand the changes and get better—even if it's different."

"I want that." Olivia felt relieved.

"Then let's make a pledge right now never to let stuff get in the middle of our friendship again—doesn't matter if it's feelings like resentment or if it's people or even geography between us."

"I'm in."

"OK. Pinkie Pledge?" Jane stood up and faced Olivia.

"Pinkie Pledge." Olivia put up both pinkie fingers and hooked Jane's pinkies just as they'd done since elementary school.

"We've never yet broken a Pinkie Pledge, you know," Jane said.

"Hmmmm. Can you remember them all?"

Jane laughed. "Well, we've never broken any I can remember."

"Do you know I prayed for you this morning?" Olivia pulled out her card and told Jane about her new quiet-time-on-the-run idea. She turned the card over. "See the happy face I stuck on there? I'll bet you know who that represents."

Jane read the verse. "Do you think maybe I need to exchange my happy face for a radiant face like in your verse?"

"Won't do you any harm." Olivia did feel radiant. The old Jane was back.

"Now that we got through all that, I want to see all your photos and hear every last detail about *Changing Faces*."

"I've been dying to tell all."

"Shall I come over tonight after dinner? We can do homework together and squeeze in every possible detail."

"OK. Mom and Dad will be happy to see you." Olivia couldn't get rid of one nagging worry, though. "What are we going to do about Aubrey?"

"I don't know. I think I'm going to try to stay friends," Jane said.

"I understand," Olivia said, and she meant it. "But will you respect my need to stay far away from her?"

"I'll try," Jane said, but she sounded anything but confident.

She knows that Aubrey cannot leave this alone.

18

"**Mia?**" Olivia tapped her on the shoulder.

She'd been standing completely still on the BART platform when Olivia came up behind her. At the sound of her name, she jumped.

"What's wrong?" It was not like Mia to be so skittish.

"I saw him."

"Saw who?"

"I saw Carlos. My stepfather."

"Where?" Olivia looked around, but the platform was deserted save for one other student.

"I'm still shaking. I know I'm not making much sense. How did he find us?"

"Come over here and sit down until the train comes." Olivia took her arms and pulled her toward an empty bench. "Now tell me."

"As I walked from school—I didn't wait for you because I thought you might get a ride with Jane. As I walked, I saw a car driving slow, looking at all the kids walking out of school. I just caught sight of the car and the driver out of the corner of my eye, but I know it was him. I ducked behind that truck by the edge of the parking lot as he drove slowly by. I saw him clearly."

"Should we call the police right now?"

"No. I don't want to take the time to find a pay phone. I want to get to the center to make sure my mother and brother are safe before we call."

"Here comes the train. Let's get on." As the train pulled to a stop and the doors automatically opened, the girls got on. It was too early for commuters yet, so the trains were nearly empty.

Mia looked around more than once before scrunching down into the seat.

"I've never seen you this shaken before."

"You don't know this man. Besides, when we call the police, it is all over for him." Mia sighed. "It's more than just a restraining order. My mother turned over papers and things—secret stuff about his smuggling business."

"To the police here?"

"Yes. She knew he would eventually come. Not because he wants us. We're property to him—he makes sure he always secures his property."

The train pulled into the Union City station. Mia

didn't talk until they were under way again. "There's too much at stake for him to let us go. We know too much."

The girls rode in silence to the next stop. They both knew that the most dangerous part of their trip would be from the station to the center.

Just before they pulled up to the Hayward station, Mia took Olivia's hands. "Dear Jesus," she prayed, "protect us. Protect my mother and my brother. Hide us under the shelter of Your wing. Amen."

"Does it seem odd to say that I felt this coming?" Mia asked.

"What do you mean?"

"I mean, our allowable time is almost up at the shelter. My mother already started looking for work, even though we knew it could be dangerous."

"I didn't know." Olivia wondered how much else Mia kept to herself.

"Plus, we knew we would need to give our references to rent an apartment. If one of our references decided to make a little money on the side, all they'd have to do is tip Carlos off."

They stepped off the train after it pulled into the Hayward station. Mia looked around carefully and pulled her hood up over her hair. "Let's go."

"Are you sure we shouldn't call the police first?" Was this foolish to go walking right into what might be a dangerous situation?

"No. I want to try to get there and warn my mother. BART runs straight through. He'd have to drive through traffic even if he knows exactly where we live. I think we'll beat him. We'll call the police from the shelter. I promise. Besides, my mother will know what to do." Mia sounded confused but determined.

Am I being foolish? Could we be walking into trouble?
Olivia put her hand over her pocket. What had her
verse said today? She didn't have time to pull it out. It
was from Genesis. Something like "Do not be afraid . . .
I am your shield." That's exactly what they needed—
a shield of protection. It also wouldn't hurt to be
shielded from sight.

They walked fast.

"Yes. I felt this coming as we moved to rebuild an in-
dependent life."

"I had no idea you were planning to leave the shelter and go out on your own. I think that's great."

They continued up the street, but Mia looked at her
with a questioning tilt of her head.

"I mean, it seems as if nobody at the shelter is in
much of a hurry to change their circumstances," Olivia
said.

They turned the corner before Mia spoke. She
clipped her words. "You've been working there almost
six months. Can you really know so little about the
people who live there?"

Olivia heard the censure in Mia's voice. "What do
you mean?"

"I remember that day when you spoke of the 'down-
and-out.' Since we became friends, I assumed you'd
come to know everyone better. Maybe I assumed too
much. Can you name me six people who live there
now?"

"Is this some kind of test?" Olivia would have ob-
jected, but the discussion helped keep the fear at bay.
They still had a few blocks to go. "Well . . . there's
Markie's mother, and then the young mom . . . I think
she's nineteen. Her baby is about six months—"

"I said 'name.'" Mia seemed angry.

"No, you're right. Maybe I can't name them." Olivia couldn't believe they were having this argument now. "My job has not been to work directly with them. In case you haven't noticed, I've been somewhat over-whelmed with the job of trying to make this benefit work."

"So, then, how do you know that none of them are 'in a hurry to change their circumstances'?" The more exasperated Mia became, the faster she walked. "You don't even know their names."

Olivia didn't answer. Why hadn't she quit? Why did she keep going in a job that only spotlighted her weakness?

"No! Please, no!" Mia halted as she looked at the steps to the shelter. From where they stopped, they could see the shattered glass on one of the double en-trance doors of the shelter. A car stood, doors open, across the sidewalk with the wheels jammed up against the shelter steps. The very position of the car suggested rage and violence.

Mia started toward the shelter, but Olivia grabbed her arm.

"Stop. If he's in there and you come up behind him, couldn't you endanger your mother and brother?"

"I need to help my mother." Mia tried to tear loose from Olivia's grip.

"As soon as the glass broke on that door, a signal went off in the police station." In fact, Olivia could hear sirens in the distance. "If you burst in, who knows what could happen?"

Mia still twisted to try to get loose.

"Think, Mia! Your stepfather could be waiting for you to show up before he takes your mother and brother."

Mia stopped trying to get free of Olivia's hand. "Yes, you may be right. I am still a missing piece for him. He always says he hates leaving loose ends. Messy."

The sirens grew louder. Olivia pulled Mia into a hedge by an auto shop. As they watched the shelter, they saw the three police cars roar up to the entrance, boxing in Carlos's car. The officers came out of their cars warily, guns drawn. One by one, they went into the shelter.

"How long sh–should we wait before—?" Mia's voice quivered with fear.

"I don't know. I guess we can go as far as the entrance. People are beginning to gather from the neighborhood."

Just then, Olivia saw Carter come out from around the back of the building and come toward where they were hiding.

She stepped out from the hedge, still clutching Mia's arm. Carter broke into a run when he saw them. When he reached them, he threw his arms around both of them.

"You're safe." He tried to slow his breathing as he stood back and looked at the two of them. "I knew you were overdue from BART, and I began to worry. I kept telling myself you'd keep a cool head and, when you saw the car and the broken glass, you'd not come barging in."

Olivia had never seen Carter so shaken.

"Come," he said. "Things are under control."

"What happened?" Mia asked. "Was it my stepfather?"

Carter nodded.

"And my mother and brother are all right?"

"Yes."

"And the police have everything under control?" Olivia asked.

"Actually, it was under control long before the police got there." Carter smiled for the first time. "If it wasn't so frightening, it would be hilarious."

"Hilarious?" Mia sounded confused.

"We'll talk later. Your mom's going to be worried sick about you, Mia. Let's go set her mind at ease. As soon as she's seen you, you'll hear everything."

Carter took both girls' hands and they walked into the middle of chaos.

"Maria Elena!" Mia's mother threw her arms around her daughter, alternating between crying and praying— between Spanish and English. "God is so good."

In the corner of the room nearest the stairs, Carlos lay facedown on the floor, arms handcuffed behind him.

"We need to talk to you," the police officer said to Mia's mother. "Can you spare us some time now?"

"You can use my office," said Mrs. Bailey. "Carter, why don't you take the girls into Diane's office. I think we need to let the police wrap things up. I had all the kids go with their families into the residences. As soon as things are back to normal, we'll all gather, so the kids can see that they are safe and secure again."

As soon as Mia sat down in Diane's chair, she started crying. "I'm s–sorry," she said. "It's just that—that now —I mean, what if Carlos is gone for good and we can start living again?"

"If I understand it correctly, Carlos will most

definitely be gone for good. I heard the police talk about smuggling and a death that was somehow connected," Carter said. "I think he's wanted for murder."

"I shouldn't be happy for all this, but the thought that we could be free . . ." Mia's voice held a note of sheer relief.

"What happened, Carter?" Olivia asked. "You said it was under control before the police even came. What do you mean? What happened?"

"You are not going to believe this," Carter said, his smile crinkling as he sat on the edge of the table. "Picture the usual after-school confusion in the reception area, only this time some of the bigger boys were playing cars with the little guys—it was worse than ever. I came in to roust the big guys into the gym at the very moment the glass shattered and a man pushed through the broken glass of the door into the room. He had a gun in his hand."

"No!" Mia covered her mouth with her hand.

"We were too surprised to be terrified at first. He seemed momentarily put off by all the kids in the room, but he screamed that he wanted his wife. He started calling your mother by name."

"Where was my brother?"

"He'd been playing cars with the bigger boys but had slipped under the desk. Your stepfather never saw him."

"Good," Mia said.

"All the kids froze," Carter said. "You would have been so proud. They could have sparked trouble with a wrong move, but instead no one spoke; no one moved."

"Had anyone ever instructed them in crisis behavior?" Olivia asked.

"I don't think so. Unfortunately, most of these kids have way too much experience with violence. Anyway, I knew Mia's mother would come out to keep him from harming anyone else. I couldn't think of a thing to do to stop it."

Mia inhaled deeply, letting the air fill her chest. The possibilities terrified her.

"I figured he needed to snatch Mia, her brother, and her mother—and run. If he left anyone, he would still be at risk. Thinking that Mia could've walked in behind him at any time further complicated things. Just as I was mulling all this over in my mind, I heard a commotion on the stairs." Carter laughed. "You know how narrow the stairs to the residence rooms are, right?"

Both girls nodded.

"There on the landing was an enormous pack of women inching down the stairs in front of your mother. They moved like one organism with dozens of legs. You should have seen Sandra, front and center, hands on her hips, practically daring him to try to get to your mother."

"No!" Mia said. "They did that for my mother?"

"Yes. Your stepfather stood there with his mouth open." Carter started laughing. "You know that Shaneece is no lightweight, either in size or in courage, right? Well, she got a little carried away and started moving toward him. In that you-better-not-be-messing-with-me voice, she started in on him. I think it went something like, 'You want a piece of this, mister?'"

"Oh, no! That could have been so dangerous, but—" Olivia couldn't help it. She burst into laughter at the picture Carter painted.

"Your stepfather was so shocked, he stepped

backward—right onto one of the kids' monster trucks—you know, Olivia, the ones that drove you crazy. It was almost like a slapstick comedy were it not for the gun and the anger."

"What happened?" Olivia did not want him to get sidetracked now.

"His feet went out from under him, and, in falling, his head hit the side of the desk and he was out for the count. As he fell, his gun slid across the room, but it didn't discharge and none of the children touched it."

Both girls sat and looked at each other.

"As Pastor Joe would say, this story has the fingerprints of God all over it." Olivia pulled her verse out of her pocket and looked at it. God did shield them.

"Anyway, that's when the police came, guns drawn," Carter said. "You know the rest."

"Shaneece, huh? And Sandra?" Olivia said the names almost to herself. How could she have come to the shelter for six months and not even known their names, let alone not known things like their courage or their you-better-not-be-messing-with-me voices?

"I'll bet you'd like to know all their names," Mia said as she draped an arm around her friend. "I'll be happy to introduce you."

"I'd consider it an honor," Olivia said. And she meant it.

✿   ✿   ✿

"Jane, I need your help with something," Olivia said into the telephone about three weeks after Mia's stepfather was arrested. "Is there any way you could come over?"

"What's wrong?"

"Nothing's wrong. I'm coming down to the wire on this benefit, and I have a wild idea that could make this an event like none other. I've been dancing around the edges of this idea for months now—"

"Dancing around? What are you talking about?"

"I mean, when I was in L.A., I kept getting twinges of an idea, but I couldn't quite get my mind around it. The feeling wouldn't leave me and now it's finally coming together. Carter and Mia are coming over, too."

"OK, you've piqued my curiosity big-time. I'm coming!"

"This is big, Jane, but we are going to keep it top secret."

"Don't say another word; picture me backing down the driveway."

Jane. Over here." Olivia waved at Jane from across the courtyard, pointing down at the bench they used for the first three years of high school. "Carter and Mia will meet us here."

"It feels funny being back on this side of the courtyard," Jane said, running her hand along the bench.

"Are you getting sentimental?"

"We had a lot of good talks on this bench."

Olivia glanced over at the senior bench. How she and Jane had longed for the day when they'd be eligible to hang out at the famed senior bench. "Remember our first day of high school when we accidentally sat on the senior bench?"

"How could I forget it," Jane said with an exaggerated shudder. "After the humiliation of that blunder, I never wanted to come back to school."

"I remember. You'd think time would soften some of those cringe-worthy memories. But then we began to talk about when the bench would be ours by right."

"It didn't turn out quite like we hoped, did it?" Jane said.

Olivia looked over at the bench and saw Aubrey walk over to it, set her things beside her, and look across the courtyard at Olivia and Jane. "No, this year kind of spiraled out of control for me."

"Yeah, and I got swept along in the spiral." Jane laughed, turning round and round, arms flailing.

How good it felt to be best friends with Jane again. All the weirdness had been talked to oblivion. They'd filled each other in on everything that had happened during the chilly times. Jane even knew every piece of furniture that had been in the Four Seasons suite, its color, and where it sat in the room. They'd spent long hours together again. The nice thing was that the hours they spent were sometimes at the shelter, where Jane dug in and helped Olivia and Mia stuff and mail letters, or at youth group, or doing homework together. Olivia found that the key to putting time into important relationships was to get your friends involved in your crazy schedule. That freed up your time to help them with theirs.

"While we wait for Carter and Mia, let me go over and say hi to Aubrey," Jane said without apology. "She gets so nervous if she's alone." Jane smiled. "Besides, I know you. When you're alone, you just open that crazy day planner or pull your quiet time out of your pocket."

"OK. Come on back when you see Carter and Mia come." As Jane left, Olivia's hand went to her jeans pocket automatically. She hadn't had time to meditate on her verse for today at all. *Please let me hear what You have to say to me today, Lord.*

She turned the card over and read: *"You have heard that it was said, 'Love your neighbor and hate your enemy.' But I tell you: Love your enemies and pray for those who persecute you, that you may be sons of your Father in heaven"* (Matthew 5:43–45).

Olivia recognized those words. They came from Jesus' Sermon on the Mount. She heard them, all right. *Sheesh!* She looked over at Aubrey talking to Jane.

When she wrote "Ignore Aubrey" in her planner all those crazy months ago, she had figured she was taking the high road—that she'd no longer play the sniping, tit-for-tat games of the past. *I guess Jesus wouldn't consider it the higher road. Love her, huh?* Olivia wanted to list all the reasons she shouldn't. After all, Aubrey was not to be trusted. She'd proved that over and over. And if she somehow figured out how to "love" Aubrey and let her hang around, wouldn't that make it look like she condoned Aubrey's shallowness?

As she looked over there again, Aubrey stepped up onto the bench in full dramatic mode, arms wide. *"If you can't love her, just start by praying for her."* Where had that thought come from? *OK, Lord, here goes: Please become real to Aubrey.* Olivia thought about that for a moment, trying to figure out what to pray for next. If God became real to Aubrey, could it fill that hole left by her mother's criticism? *Father, help Aubrey know she's precious in Your sight even if she's never been precious in her mom's sight.* Olivia felt tears prick her eyelids. *Lord, what is that? Why am I crying for Aubrey?*

She wiped her eyes quickly before Carter and Mia saw. They were walking toward her from the cafeteria. Jane waved good-bye to Aubrey and came walking over as well. Olivia saw the slight drop of Aubrey's shoulders. *This must feel as if I've "won" again to her.*

Olivia had an idea. *God, help me, please.* "Hang tight for a second, guys. I need to enlist the help of one more specialist for Operation Angels' Wings."

Olivia walked across the courtyard. "Aubrey, would you be willing to join our transformation team?"

Aubrey seemed wary. "Is this some kind of a joke?"

"No. Far from it. We've taken on a huge challenge, and we need your eye."

"My eye? What are you talking about?" Aubrey's bracelets clinked together as she took her finger and nervously wound it in her hair.

"No one can style a fashion look like you. Come on over. Let us tell you what we're planning and then see if we don't need you."

Aubrey looked over to Jane standing with Carter and Mia. "I guess I can listen."

It was a start, anyway.

"OK, gather round. This is an official meeting of the Transformation Team for Operation Angels' Wings." Olivia jumped right into the meeting as soon as she and Aubrey joined the group.

"I asked Aubrey to join us because there is no one at Bay Vista who can put together a look better than

206

Aubrey. We need her help. I'm going to put her with Maree. She's the editor of *Spree,* Aubrey."

"I know who Maree Moore is, and I know what *Spree* is." Aubrey put her hands up toward the sky. "Will someone kindly tell me what Operation Angels' Wings is?"

"Can someone explain it to Aubrey? You have to promise, though, to keep this top secret."

Aubrey blinked hard a couple times as if puzzled. "Why would you trust me with your secrets, Olivia? I mean, we do have a history together, and it's not been pretty."

"Jane thinks you're something special, so I'm trusting her judgment. Besides, we really do need you. Jane, tell her why."

Jane filled in all the details with Mia popping in to add bits and pieces. Aubrey's face gave them their first clue that they'd hit pay dirt with Operation Angels' Wings.

"Is it brilliant or what?" Jane asked.

"Fantastic," said Aubrey, mimicking Jane.

Everyone laughed. Jane and Mia took turns filling Aubrey in on some of the logistical things.

When Olivia looked up, she noticed Carter looking intently at her. *What?*

He continued to look at her, and when he smiled his eyes crinkled into a tender look.

Olivia was bewildered. *What was that about?*

When Carter saw that Olivia didn't understand, he nodded slightly toward Aubrey and then gave a subtle thumbs-up signal to Olivia.

She savored this private moment while the others talked. He was glad she had reached out to Aubrey.

"OK, everyone, time to wrap up here. I have your assignments for the weeks leading up to the benefit." Olivia handed out instructions and schedules. "Aubrey, I need to get yours done and to put you in contact with Maree."

"I get to speak to Maree Moore myself?"

"Sure. One thing I've learned this year is that the only way I'm going to accomplish everything is to twist the arms of the best people I know. I'm counting on each one of you to handle your areas."

"Aye, aye, Captain," said Jane as she saluted and clicked her heels.

Olivia rolled her eyes. "Because of Operation Angels' Wings, the *Changing Faces* crew will be here two days early to get rolling."

"Does Diane know?" Carter asked.

"No. Kinni and the producer think Diane's surprise might be one of the strongest story lines for our episode. Diane doesn't think they are coming until the morning of the benefit. That's when they originally planned to style me and prepare for the reveal."

"When she comes in on Saturday morning, she is going to die!" Jane said.

Carter winced but quickly recovered. "Jane, can you manage to find a better term? We're still celebrating Diane's recovery, you know."

"Yikes," Jane said, wrinkling her nose. "You know me and language—never exactly spot-on."

"Do you want to hear how successful we are?" Olivia asked. "Because of the *Changing Faces* involvement, we are already completely sold out of tickets to the benefit. Mrs. Bailey is so excited. Plus, thanks to our quick-thinking Mia, we offered photo ops with

Kinni for any of our guests willing to fork up an extra donation."

"I suggested we leave the donation amount up to them," Mia said. "That turned out to be my best idea yet. They've pledged far more than we'd have ever dared to ask."

"Then, before the dinner begins, we'll do a silent auction for the privilege of having the famous Kinni McKay seated at the winner's table for the whole evening." Olivia smiled as she shook her head. "Kinni's such a good sport, and she's just as determined to raise money as we are. I have the servers prepared to add a table setting to the winning table as soon as the auction ends."

Carter laughed and put his hand over his back pocket. "I think I'd better sew my wallet into my pocket around this group."

"What do you mean?" Jane put her hand on her hip and batted her eyelashes in an outrageous way. "We put the fun in fund-raising."

"OK, team," Olivia said as the bell rang. "Don't forget, we have our makeovers scheduled first thing on that Thursday morning. That's so the local team pulled together by *Changing Faces* gets a chance to see how to work multiple makeovers. It'll also give the cameramen a chance to see how they want to shoot it."

"You mean we'll have makeovers and get to appear on the show?" Aubrey asked.

"Yep," Carter said. "Even me."

Real TV

Operation Angels' Wings

Bring the truck around the back, Philip." Carter gestured with his arm as he directed traffic. "Now that it's completely unloaded, we can get it out of the way."

Mrs. Bailey stood with Olivia. "This is amazing—truly amazing."

"I know. When we decided on Operation Angels' Wings as our code name for this project, who ever thought we'd have so many human 'angels' work so hard to give wings to all our dreams?" Olivia still couldn't believe it. "When will Diane be here?"

"Joe's on his way with her now. All I can say is that it's a good thing the benefit is completely set up at the hotel ballroom—this place is a madhouse."

"Are all the residents ready for the special reveal?" Olivia asked.

"I think everything's ready, but who knows? The children are so excited, the moms will be exhausted by the time we call them." Mrs. Bailey moved over toward the door. "There's Diane now."

As Diane walked into the reception area, she wore a puzzled expression. "Hello, everyone." She came over to Olivia. "What's going on? I figured there'd be quiet music and I'd catch the last of your makeup session. It's utter chaos here!"

"It is, isn't it?" Mrs. Bailey said. The smile plastered across her face should have given it away.

"Why are there three huge trucks out there—one with the *Changing Faces* logo and two rental trucks?" Diane walked around. "Olivia, I'm totally confused. What's going on? I read your schedules and every brief you sent me. This looks nothing like any of it."

The cameras were rolling and one cameraman pulled in tight to Diane and Olivia. Diane automatically put her hand up to her short, curly hair.

"We have a few surprises for you, Diane." Olivia gave her a reassuring hug. She could see that Diane's bewildered look only deepened. "Remember the original plans we discussed?"

"Yes. I have them right here." Diane held out a folder full of papers.

Olivia took the folder out of her hand and flung it over her shoulder. Papers fluttered to the floor. "Those plans are obsolete." Olivia knew the camera would love that visual.

"First, let me introduce you to Kinni McKay." Olivia gestured toward the staircase where Kinni made an entrance.

Kinni took over as she came and put an arm around Diane. "Diane Javier first wrote to us almost a year ago, suggesting we do a makeover for her so that the shelter and its work could be spotlighted. We thought it was an excellent idea." Kinni invited Diane to sit with her on the designer couch that *Changing Faces* had trucked in for the impromptu set. "When we wrote to invite her on the show, we learned of her recent diagnosis of breast cancer. It looks like she's won her battle, but Diane wrote us a funny, poignant letter to say that she was somewhat hair-challenged at the moment and would we take her young volunteer assistant."

Kinni put out her hand to indicate that Olivia should come over and join them. "Had I known what we were in for, I'm not sure we would have signed on. You've all met Olivia in her before-photos and in her *Changing Faces* makeover. What you don't know is that Olivia can enlist people to her cause better than anyone I've ever met."

Olivia blushed.

"When she came down to Hollywood, she first convinced us to bring a whole crew here for the reveal, so we could really highlight the work of the shelter. Right, Olivia?"

"The idea began to grow as we talked," Olivia said. "And don't let Kinni tell you I twisted arms at *Changing Faces*. The *Changing Faces* team has hearts of gold. They signed on early, and they stayed excited the whole time."

"Diane," Kinni said, "we've scheduled you for a full makeover this afternoon, but first I want to show you what we've been doing here at The Shelter of His Wing since late Wednesday night."

"Wednesday night?" Diane turned toward Olivia. "Wednesday night?"

"Cut," yelled the director. "OK, get that couch turned around. Have it face the stairs. Ladies, step over here for a moment."

"Fess up, missy," Diane said with a huge grin, putting her hands on her hips. "What are you up to?"

"Remember how I told you I lacked the gift of mercy and I wasn't suited for this work? That was nothing more than an excuse, though I didn't understand that then. As I first got to know Mia and then came to see the courage and strength of the residents, I saw that it wasn't about a volunteer showing mercy to the 'down-and-out.' How ridiculous!" Olivia closed her eyes and shook her head in a shudder. "I had far more to learn from them than they could ever get from me."

"Sounds like it was an eye-opener."

"You have no idea," Olivia continued. "So, when I saw the warehouse at the *Changing Faces* studio, the wheels began to turn, but it wasn't until I witnessed the lives changing here at the shelter that I got the whole brainstorm."

"Oh, boy. I think I'm in for it."

"I hope you like your surprise. *Changing Faces* is using it for a ninety-minute special—that's why all this extra footage—"

"Let's roll." Michael directed Kinni and Diane to sit on the couch again. Olivia stood over by the staircase.

"Let me first introduce our team," Olivia said. "We

called ourselves the Transformation Team. First, meet Carter Wylie. He headed up logistical support." Olivia told a little about Carter's work at the shelter and had Carter introduce Philip and the rest of the behind-the-scenes people.

"This is Maria Elena, but we call her Mia. She handled all the details of setting this up and enlisting community support." Olivia let Mia introduce Mrs. Bailey and the others from the shelter.

"And meet Aubrey Ainsley." Olivia looked over at Diane to see her eyes widen at Aubrey being included in a project of Olivia's. "Aubrey worked with Maree Moore of *Spree*. . . ." Olivia had Aubrey and Maree introduce the small army of local fashion people they used for the project.

"And finally, meet Jane, my right hand and best friend. Jane worked with hairstylist Steef and makeup artist Bianca to set up local talent by the dozens to help us pull this off in a day and a half."

Jane, Steef, and Bianca introduced almost twenty local stylists and makeup artists.

"And . . . cut," Michael said. "There. That worked out well. I'm not sure how we'll work all that in—it's a lot of intros, but that's the fun of this huge project, right?"

One of the hairstylists spoke up. "It's our pleasure. We were more than happy to donate our services. This *Changing Faces* gig is going to look impressive on my résumé." All the stylists laughed.

"Will someone tell me what is going on?" Diane wailed. "Joe, did you know about this?"

Pastor Joe pretended to look guilty and ducked out of the room, to the delight of all.

"OK," Michael said, waving his arms for quiet. "Are we all ready for the mass reveal?"

"Ready," everyone said in unison.

"Let's roll."

Music faded in and Kinni stood by the staircase. "First, we have Sandra," she said, holding her arm out, palm up, toward the staircase. "You can see from her before-photos that Sandra needed a little polishing before she was ready to take her place in the workforce."

Diane looked at Olivia with eyes wide open.

She could tell that Diane now understood. They had amassed this whole army of fashion stylists to do makeovers on every single resident of the shelter. It took three trucks to bring all the fashions and accessories that Aubrey and Maree would need to choose from in order to create clothing makeovers for the women.

Later, when the show aired, Diane would see what fun they all had doing the makeovers. The two days were filled with laughter and heartfelt tears. The stylists had enjoyed it as much as the women. Shouts of "Mommy, you look beautiful," still echoed throughout the shelter. And tonight—like Cinderella going to her ball—all the ladies would be guests at the benefit. As Mia said, it wouldn't hurt them one bit to meet some of the leading Bay Area businesspeople.

Olivia couldn't wait to see the final show after all the chaos landed on the cutting-room floor and the camera focused on the changing faces.

Yes. This surprise was worth all the subterfuge we went through. Olivia squeezed Diane's hand as Sandra came down the stairs to a chorus of delighted laughs and clapping. She looked wonderful. Her hair had been expertly cut and styled. She wore a sweater set and skirt and carried a jacket over her arm.

"Sandra's skills should be able to land her a job in an office," Kinni said. "With her new wardrobe and up-to-the-minute look, we think she'll be a real asset to any firm."

"Cut."

☆   ☆   ☆

Late that night, Diane sat with the worn-out team—Olivia, Jane, Carter, Mia, and Aubrey—around one of the tables. "I can't believe how exhausted I am."

"But, boy, do you look good," Jane said. "I love the way they moussed your hair and crisped it up. And the way they did your eyes—you look mah-velous, dahling."

"Actually, we all look pretty good," Carter said. "And coming from me, that's high praise."

Carter sat right next to Olivia. He looked good—no question—but his before-shots looked awfully good to Olivia already. *It's tough to improve on Carter.*

"Well, it was a success—hands down," Diane said. "Olivia's parents and Joe are still working with Mrs. Bailey to get a rough accounting before we head home, but it's more than double what we've done before."

Diane took Olivia's hands. "No one can organize like you, and no one can put a team together like you." She let go of Olivia's hands and spoke to the others, "But that's not to take anything away from any of you—you were all amazing."

She continued in a soft voice, "But I just wanted to say that nothing has ever touched me like seeing our women come down those stairs, one by one. I don't think we'll ever know the impact this has had on their lives."

"Olivia, what made you decide to share the makeover experience with everyone at the shelter?" Aubrey asked.

"It was Mia's words that made me reexamine myself. When the interviewer asked her about homelessness, she used the verse about 'where your treasure is, there your heart will be.' And then she said her treasure was in people—her mother and brother—not in things." Olivia paused for a moment. "I couldn't stop thinking about it. I had made my accomplishments, my schedule, and my planner my treasure. I didn't even see the people until they stood there protecting Mia's mom the day of the break-in." She shook her head. "What an eye-opener."

Carter put his finger to his lips, then gently touched Olivia's nose. "I can't call her 'Chip' anymore. In fact, I can't even find the remnant of a chip on this shoulder," he teased. "Everyone keeps remarking about how beautiful everyone looks tonight. I think Olivia's as beautiful inside as she is on the outside."

Jane just rolled her eyes. "Brilliant, Carter, that's just what we all needed to hear."

Carter just smiled that crinkly smile that Olivia loved.

✿   ✿   ✿

A week later, Olivia still hadn't slowed down.

As she slammed her locker to head out to the parking lot with an early release hall pass in hand, Jane caught up with her. "What are you thinking? You can't leave now. They are going to announce our valedictorian at three o'clock."

Olivia stopped for a minute and then laughed. "I can't believe I'm saying this, but you know what I just realized? It no longer matters. Nope, it really doesn't matter at all." She hugged a startled Jane and took off at a run to meet Carter so they could help Mia and her family make the move to their very own house.

And she meant what she said—it no longer mattered. She'd finally gotten the makeover she needed and, in the process, found her real treasure.

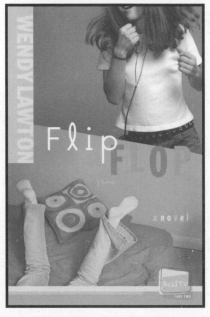

Daughters of the Faith series, for ages 8-12

A story based on the life of holocaust survivor, Anita Dittman.

Shadow of His Hand
ISBN: 0-8024-4074-6

A story based on the life of Mary Bunyan, the daughter of John Bunyan.

The Tinker's Daughter
ISBN: 0-8024-4099-1

A story based on the life of Mary Chilton, a young girl from Holland who traveled to America on the Mayflower.

Almost Home
ISBN: 0-8024-3637-4

A story based on the life of Pioneer Olive Oatman.

Ransom's Mark
ISBN: 0-8024-3638-2

A story based on the life of Harriet Tubman, who was freed from slavery through the Underground Railroad.

Courage to Run
ISBN: 0-8024-4098-3

A story based on the life of Salvation Army Pioneer Eliza Shirley.

The Hallelujah Lass
ISBN: 0-8024-4073-8

S INCE 1894, Moody Publishers has been dedicated to equip and motivate people to advance the cause of Christ by publishing evangelical Christian literature and other media for all ages, around the world. Because we are a ministry of the Moody Bible Institute of Chicago, a portion of the proceeds from the sale of this book go to train the next generation of Christian leaders.

If we may serve you in any way in your spiritual journey toward understanding Christ and the Christian life, please contact us at www.moodypublishers.com.

"All Scripture is God-breathed and is useful for teaching, rebuking, correcting and training in righteousness, so that the man of God may be thoroughly equipped for every good work."
—*2 TIMOTHY 3:16, 17*

MOODY
PUBLISHERS

THE NAME YOU CAN TRUST®

CHANGING FACES TEAM

ACQUIRING EDITOR
Michele Straubel

COPY EDITOR
Cessandra Dillon

BACK COVER COPY
Becky Armstrong

COVER DESIGN
UDG DesignWorks, Inc.

COVER PHOTO
Photodisc

INTERIOR DESIGN
Ragont Design

PRINTING AND BINDING
Bethany Press International

The typeface for the text of this book is
Giovanni